THE
ASSASSIN

LINDA BRANSGROVE

Copyright © 2022 Linda Bransgrove.

All rights reserved. No part of this book may be reproduced, stored, or transmitted by any means—whether auditory, graphic, mechanical, or electronic—without written permission of both publisher and author, except in the case of brief excerpts used in critical articles and reviews. Unauthorized reproduction of any part of this work is illegal and is punishable by law.

This Book Is Entirely Fictional. Any Names of People Living or Dead Bearing The Same Name Is Purely Coincidental.

PROLOGUE

THE ASSASSIN BOARDED THE PLANE WITH A SENSE OF SATISFACtion. They had got through customs okay with their plastic gun in tow. It only fired one bullet but they felt a sense of safety knowing it was there. Their handler had given them this assignment and a list of sources for information to find their mark. One assassin had tried already and failed. They knew what that meant. Another assassin would be sent to kill them. This Assassin hadn't relied on all the sources given them, having gathered a network of their own over the years. They had been given the job because they had built up a reputation of never failing. They had no intention of failing. It was not in their code. They would fulfil their mission then get paid and go abroad, somewhere hot. Living in the USA was great but they needed a break. One day, they would have made enough money to retire. That's if they could retire. Meantime, the chase was on.......

ROBERT JOHNSON WAS IN THE WRONG PLACE AT THE WRONG time. He had witnessed a brutal murder and got a good look at the guy who had done it. He had immediately got out his cell phone and rung the Police. When they arrived, they wanted him to go to headquarters with them to look through a book of known felons. He quickly rang his wife Beth to tell her that he would be late home.

At headquarters, he was given a book of photographs to look through in hope that he may recognise the man he had seen. After a while he found the man.

"We've been after this guy for a long time. Are you willing to give evidence in a court of law?"

"I'll give it a go."

"We have to warn you he has a network of gang members. Your life and that of your family will be in danger. Talk it over with your family and ring me in the morning."

"I'll do that". He got up and made his way home.

"I just hope the Gang members don't get to him first," said Captain Bedford to the records clerk.

Robert drove home stunned and shaking. The fact that the car was automatic made it easier. When he got home, he was still shaking and couldn't speak.

"Whatever has happened to you?" asked Beth. Robert got the family together and told them he had been to Police headquarters.

"He's in shock" said Josephine. "Mom, get some coffee." Beth did so.

"What happened?" asked Beth.

"I saw a guy kill a guy inside that old factory on Ninth Street. I saw his face and called the Police. I've looked through some photos and they want me to identify him in a line-up tomorrow."

"I don't like the sound of it," said Beth "but if this man has been getting away with murder someone has to stand up to him. Girls, what do you think? It could be very dangerous and I don't want anything to happen to you."

"You have to do what you think is right. I have to admit I'm scared," said Joanna. "Yeah, same here," said Josephine. "I really don't want some creep following me or worse".

"It's a really hard decision," said Robert "but I saw what he did. He cut the guy's throat."

"Yuk" said the girls.

"It's an awful position to be in," said Robert. "I'm scared for us all but I think I should do the right thing, I hope you all understand."

"We do," said the girls and Beth nodded her assent.

"We're all behind you Robert," said Beth.

Morning came and they sat down to a stack of pancakes with maple syrup in silence. It was the first time that had happened. Usually the family were buzzing about something or other. Robert broke the silence when they had all eaten.

"Well, I guess I'd better ring the Police and let them know my decision." He picked up the phone and began to dial.

Captain Bedford picked up the phone. "Yeah?"

"It's Robert Johnson, I've decided to go ahead. We talked it over and whilst I want to keep my family safe, I think I should do it."

"Thank you Robert. Here's what we do. We bring him in and put him in a lineup. We put you behind a one-way mirror so the guys in the lineup can't see you. They're all holding numbers so you just have to pick out the number of the guy you saw then we take them all out and arrest the one you picked out providing it was the right one. You'll be taken out of the area before they are moved so don't worry. We'll call you when everything is ready this end. Try not to worry I know it's hard but you'll be taking a very dangerous criminal off the streets."

"I worry for my family."

"I understand. We'll offer what protection we can."

Two days later Robert got a call from the Police.

"We'd like you to come to the station. Would this afternoon be okay for you?"

"I'll have to check with my boss."

"Give me their number. I'll call them." He did that.

An hour later Robert got the call. He made his way there with some apprehension but also with a sense of peace. He parked his car and entered the station.

"Right," said Captain Bedford. "Follow me. It's just this way".

He was led into a room with a one-way mirror. Robert looked closely at all of those in the lineup.

"Number five" he said without hesitation.

"Okay Mr Johnson thank you for your help today".

He led him out then barked to his officers "It's number five. Get that animal out of here and put him in a cage where he belongs!"

"I'm allowed a phone call," yelled Big Al.

"Give him the phone," yelled one of the officers.

"Roger, find out who may testify. Find out where the wife works and do what we've done before. I want him stopped! Get our attorney in too."

"Will do," said Roger. "Leave it with me. Yeah, ok Al, will do." The noise in the cell hid his conversation.

Robert made his way to the office. He worked in Special Intelligence in the Secret Service. He told his family he worked for the Government. He was listening to chatter from terrorists and hacking his way into their computers. They had foiled many attempts against the States and kept London appraised of any headed their way. It was a mutual effort, and over the years they had got to know a number of fellow agents.

TWO WEEKS LATER

Beth was in the classroom where she taught a math lesson which had gone well, when one of the students stood up with a gun in his hand. The girls screamed. Beth turned from the board she was writing on. She had had training in what to do in a situation like this but had never actually have it happen to her.

"Fraser," she tried to keep her voice from shaking. "What are you doing?"

"I got this gun, see, and you all have to do what I tell you. Get on the floor all a' you."

They did as he said but Beth could see his eyes were wild. He was waving the gun all over the place. She prayed he wouldn't pull the trigger. He looked as though he was on drugs. He sprayed some bullets into the window. It broke and splinters of glass went everywhere. Some hit some of the children. Beth prayed he had spent all of them. The surrounding classes would have heard and would raise the alarm.

"I'm the King of the class," raved Fraser. He pulled the trigger again this time aiming it at one of his class mates who was a real bully and constantly bullied Fraser. The gun clicked. It was empty.

"Thank God," said Beth and got up from the floor. "Susie Shaw please go and get Mr Trent for me, thank you." Susie ran out of the class room to do as she'd been asked. "Every-one out please, in an orderly fashion, no running, please line up in the corridor. Some-one will come and take you to the hall where you can wait safely."

She sat down at her desk. Fraser was sitting at his desk now.

"I was King of the class. Why did the gun run out of bullets?"

Beth knew she had to keep him calm. He was obviously on some kind of drug. Before she could speculate further, Mr Trent entered the room. He had dealt with this kind of thing many times over the years, too many times.

"Beth you can go", he said. "I can take it from here".

"Thank you," said Beth. She got her coat and left the building, got into her car and once she felt more settled, headed for home.

The girls had already arrived home when she got there and so had Robert. They had been notified. He held out his arms and Beth felt his comforting touch and the tears came.

"Thank God you were all safe", he said. "It could have been much worse. I'm so glad you're home safe". He hugged her tightly and just let her cry. By now, the girls were crying too. "Family hug" said Robert. They all made a circle and hugged each other, and cried until they were spent.

Later that evening, Mr Trent rang Beth.

"Fraser had taken drugs. He's in Police custody. You might like to know the girls who were injured didn't have any deep wounds, they won't be left with any deep scars. They are pretty shaken up of course. Are you okay?"

"Yes, I'm feeling better now, thank you. I admit it threw me at the time. I've not dealt with that situation before."

"Well, I'm just glad you're safe. See you tomorrow."

"'Bye, and thanks for calling." She relayed the news to her family. It rang again shortly after she had put it down. "That was Captain Bedford. The gun had a bullet left but the gun jammed."

"Oh Mom", said Joanna "to think someone could have died is awful."

"He said there's more to the story and he would call around this evening."

Sure enough at seven pm there was a ring on the door. "Hello Mrs Johnson I hope I'm not disturbing you".

"No that's fine. Do come in. This way." She led him to the living room.

"Fraser is being interviewed by the Juvenile detectives. I brought along a copy of his statement so far. I'd better just read it to you. They are still interviewing him but they are having a hard time. We think there's more he's hiding but here's what we have so far:-

> "I met this man see who told me I was a very special person. I ain't had nobody say that to me before. Well, he gets out this stuff some pills I think and says he has a very special job for me to do and the pills would help me to do it 'cos they'd make me feel good. Then he gets out this money and it was fifty dollars. I ain't never had fifty dollars so I says to him what is it all about, seeing that I was confused like. Then he gets out this gun. "You ever shot a gun?" he says. Sure, I go hunting with my Dad I says. That's good we thought we'd found the right kid for the job. See a man called Big Al is in court 'cos of Mr Johnson. He wants to send a message to Mr Johnson. You take the pills on the day you choose to do it. They'll make you feel really good as if you can do anything. Here's what Big Al wants you to do when you're next in Mrs Johnson's class. Take the pills a half hour before the class. They act fast so be careful. Then

halfway through the class you should feel like the King of the world. Take out the gun and aim it at Mrs Johnson's arm or leg. We don't want her dead, it's just a message we're sending to Mr Johnson. Big Al's gang will be doing the rest later. Well Sir I did like he said and the pills did make me feel wonderful but when it came to shooting Mrs Johnson I couldn't, I like her, so I aimed the gun at Zak. I hate him. He bullies me so I go to shoot him but the gun wouldn't fire. May be for the best 'cos I would a been done for murder they tell me. He wanted me to tell Mr Johnson and you there's nowhere he can't reach you this is just the start."

"It makes chilling reading I know. We are trying to find out from Fraser where the man came from and what he looks like. We're trying to get a sketch artist to help get a picture of him if Fraser can't pick him out from the photo book."

"I feel like I'm living in a bad dream" said Beth.

"What have I done to my family?" said Robert. "I've put us at risk. Isn't there anything you can do Captain?"

"I'm afraid not. At least not at this stage. He actually has to harm you before we can do more."

"Look," said Robert "what if Fraser had done the job?"

"We still can't touch him unless we get the man Fraser met. That's what we're trying to do but I have to warn you it won't be easy. They know how to keep out of reach."

"So, we're stuck with it. Why did I testify, why? We're in harm's way now 24/7. What do you advise us to do?"

"Get outside lights that come on if someone is there, get a

good alarm system as this is a house and if you don't have one get a gun and have lessons both of you and for your daughters too."

"I have a gun Beth and I know how to use it. We'll get lessons for the girls."

THREE WEEKS LATER

Robert was told that Alfred Jones was going to be in court the next day.

"It's been fast tracked as we'd been after him for some time. There was a court cancellation. We've had witnesses before but they've been got at. I'm surprised you didn't get the same treatment, but I'm glad you didn't. We need to get him put away."

"We have been got at but I'll still be there. What time is it?"

"Three p.m."

"Right." He drove to the court and met the Captain.

"How were you got at?" Robert told him. "Oh boy that's nasty. Are you sure you want to go ahead?"

"Yes, I will."

"I warn you, they'll grill you hard but I think you'll cope well. You strike me as a man who can take pressure."

It was his job of course but he guessed they knew that. One of the guys at work had been keeping watch for any problems. "I hope I can do enough to get him put away. I can't forget what I saw. It was horrific."

After two hours it was all over. Alfred had been found guilty and given a sentence on death row.

"I'll get you for this", he had ranted. "I'll have you killed. I warned you off with your wife being shot at but you still took no notice. You're a dead man!" Then had come a sentence of expletives and "I've seen your face see, you're a dead man."

Robert didn't doubt he'd done that to other people who had got in his way or who had 'crossed' him.

"Thank you for your help," said Captain Bedford. "It sure helps to get him off the streets."

"Yeah, after what I saw he's going to be in the right place."

"I'm really grateful to you, you want a ride home or did you drive?"

"I drove thanks."

"Okay I'll let you get home".

Robert drove home after having texted Beth. It felt good to know the guy was off the streets but he couldn't help being concerned for his family. He had seen danger in his job but it was another thing living it!

A letter later arrived in the post. It read: "From now on your life will be hell! Big Al wants you scared, and we're gonna make it happen!"

Robert rang Captain Bedford and read the letter to him.

"I'll have a car drive past your house, that's the best I can do at this stage. If it gets bad let me know".

Robert told his family to be on guard. "Girls, be careful when you're driving or stopping for gas."

"We can ask the church for prayer when we go on Sunday", said Beth.

"Yes, right," said Robert, "we'll do that."

They settled down to watch a movie. Both girls were in for the night, Joanna's boyfriend having to work late. He worked in the Hospital as a surgeon. Joanna had met Craig at work, as she was a Nurse, as was Josephine. The girls had elected to stay with their parents, despite them being old enough to "leave the nest". They had told their parents there was no point in them leaving when they only had a twenty-minute drive to the Hospital. They enjoyed the movie and were getting ready for bed when a note was put through the door and the doorbell rang. Robert went out to investigate. The note read: "This will be you. Look outside." He did so and a dead animal had been left to the step. He had to tell the family and warned them again. He disposed of the animal.

They all went out to their respective jobs in the morning. It was a beautiful day and not one for work but they had to do it. Joanna worked as a surgical nurse while Josephine worked in ICU. Joanna managed to catch up with Craig. They took their lunch outside. "Hey."

"Hey yourself", said Craig. Are you working at the weekend? I'm off."

"As it happens, Honey, I'm off too."

"That's great, we can do something special."

"Sure, it'll be good to do something like that. I have to tell you what's going on in my family."

He held her hand. "What is it Jo?"

"My Dad gave evidence against a brutal murderer. Now his gang are making threats against Dad. They tried to shoot Mom at school. They want my Dad dead. We've had threats and a dead animal was left outside last night."

"Oh Honey," He put his arms around her and held her close "That's really awful. We see enough of what guns can do in our jobs, I sure don't want to see your Dad on the table or you."

"It feels like a bad dream, one you hope you'll wake up from."

"We'll have a good weekend and try to enjoy it Jo but I'm scared for you and your family. Can't the Police do something?"

"They're sending a car to keep circling our home."

"Not a lot then." He looked at his watch. "Sorry, I have to get back." "Me too", said Jo. They hugged and kissed then went back into the Hospital building.

Meanwhile, Robert had explained to his Boss what was going on. His Boss asked the Team to keep an eye out. "He's one of our own, look out for him". Robert appreciated their support and told them so.

"It's a bit like a movie at the moment, so unreal, but I take this guy seriously, he's really evil. My main concern is for my family but I don't regret testifying." "Understood," said his Boss. "The Police know you are working for the Government. We'll get their co-operation."

"Thanks to all of you."

His Boss put an arm around him. "We're like a second family Rob, we're on it". Robert felt a lump in his throat.

"I'd better get some work done". He sat at his desk and fired up his computer. It was all he could do to hold back the tears.

The Assassin was making good progress. They would have to change planes soon but they figured their last informant's report had been useful. It would take a while to get to the next informant. When they disembarked, there would be the informant somewhere in the airport. They both had "burn" pay-as-you-go cheap, not registered, phones. They would contact each other then toss the phone away. The informant knew they couldn't risk being seen. Some Assassins hunted them down and shot them so they were taking no chances. The Assassin had spent some time in the Army. It was there that they had honed all their skills in self-defence and using guns. They had served in Afghanistan and left the army after that. It was the usual story. There was no work for a soldier who was in "civvy" street. They had joined the local Gun Club and their skills proved to be an asset. After a number of weeks, they became aware that someone was watching them. A few weeks later someone else joined the first person in the watching. Feeling disconcerted, they were determined that they would do something. They moved fast around the back of the course that was full of wooden "people" that popped up randomly and were either a 'good' or a 'bad person.' The aim was to get around the course as fast as possible, ducking and diving, and shooting only the bad guys. Then they sprinted to where they were out of sight and aimed to get as far behind the men as possible. There wasn't much room on the stand but they shot up behind them and tapped them on the shoulder.

"What the heck do you think you're doing, watching me? I don't like it! Can you please stop it!"

One of the men had turned with a look of amusement on his face.

"This is no place to talk. There's hardly any room to move here. I suggest the diner down the road. It has outdoor tables. We can explain there if you're interested?"

"I guess it won't hurt to listen."

"It will be to your advantage I assure you."

"Okay, I'll listen.

They had followed them to the diner and one of the men selected a table. The bulk of diners were inside. Only a couple of tables were taken. They ordered coffee then one of the men said:

"We've been watching you for a reason. You have skill sets that would help us very much and the money is good."

"All right, so I'm interested. What's the catch?"

Then they laid out on the table a piece of paper with the figure for becoming an Assassin. It was more money than they had ever seen.

"Here are the terms if you decide to take up our offer. You'll be given a picture of the person we want killed by your Handler. He or she will give you a list of our trusted informers. You'll arrange to meet using burn phones which you destroy when the information is given. When you kill the Mark take a photo with the Polaroid- Camera we give you. Take a photo of the dead Mark then put it in the envelope that's already addressed and stamped then pop it in the post. You get half the money before you go to cover your expenses and the rest will be wired direct to your bank account on completion. You have to let us know by seven pm this evening. We hope we will have the pleasure of you joining us."

They got up to leave. "What happens if I say no?"

"You become the Mark."

They were stunned. The men left leaving them shaking and conflicted. They had no choice by the sound of it. They felt like ice and couldn't move for shaking. It was one thing to kill on the battle field but this was in cold blood. Their mind was spinning and they thought back to their family.

They had lived in Montana and loved climbing the well-used trails. They had gone hunting with their Pa and could never bring themselves to shoot a living animal. They had had a good upbringing. Their parents were of the middle class and they had been to a good school where their sporting capabilities were soon picked up on and used. They had opted to join the army on leaving school and it had been a good choice. Sure, it was hard going with all the discipline, it was all hard work but they had also gained other skills like repairing cars and lorries. All in all it had made them the person they were today. Their parents had been proud of them. What would they think now? Their skills had painted them into a corner. It was as well their parents were both dead. They had been driving home and were forced off the road by some drunk driver and tumbled to their death over the cliff beside it. It was hard losing them both at the same time. It was partly the reason they had left the army a bit early. They needed time to grieve and there was no time for that on the battle field. They pulled themselves up from the table and tried to make their legs work. They were going to have to treat it as dispassionately as they could. They got to their home and flung their jacket over a chair. The wall clock said five to seven. They didn't know how they had driven home - it had been a reflex action to drive perhaps, they didn't know. Seven o'clock. They took out the card one of the men had given them and began to dial. The phone rang twice then was picked up. They told them their name and their decision was to agree to do it.

"Good, good. We really didn't want to see someone with your skills disposed of. We'll be in touch in a week, we have to arrange for your Handler and further details. You will only have one Handler given to you. We find continuity works best. So glad you're joining us. Goodbye."

The Assassin didn't usually drink but they needed something. They grabbed a bottle of scotch, filled a glass and sat down. It seemed like a bad dream or a horror movie. They drained the glass then had another. There was nothing they could do except die themselves, they'd had no choice. Their head felt heavy - the scotch had made them feel sleepy. They leaned back into the chair and let the oblivion of sleep claim them. They would deal with it in the morning. They woke up in the morning with a headache and headed for the medicine cupboard for some Tylenol. They downed some then started to make breakfast. In the cold light of day things looked different. They struggled with their conscience and the fact that they could do the job. The first one would be the hardest but they would have to overcome it and think of it as they had in the army. It was either them or their life would be taken. They ate their breakfast still thinking it through. They may as well make some money. Their parents had left them their home which they lived in now, and some money from a life insurance they'd had. They knew their parents would have been horrified had they lived. They had been good parents and had brought them up lovingly. There was a safety deposit box in the bank that they had left to be opened only after their deaths. The Assassin had never got around to going to the bank and there wouldn't be time now. Just then the postman rang the doorbell.

"I have a package for you. Could you sign here please?"

They signed then took the package and laid it on the table. Inside was a letter asking them to ring a certain number in the next twenty-four hours and to use the codeword "Assassin." Also there was a Polaroid Camera. All the mystery involved in this was doing their head in. May as well get the thing done, they thought. They picked up the phone and began to dial. An automated voice asked for the codeword. They said "Assassin" then waited.

"Just putting you through" said the voice again. "Hello" said a machine altered voice. "You'll be our latest addition to the family. Welcome. Can you come to this address at four p.m.? We have a client for you."

"I can come now if you want."

"Ah, eagerness, I like that, yes do. You got the address written down?"

"Yes."

"Then I look forward to meeting you soon." They put down the phone and steadied their shaking hand. Picking up their jacket they headed for the address given.

They were at the address waiting. Shortly a screen lit up with a distorted picture of someone. Again, the voice had been altered.

"Welcome to our newest recruit. We have been apprised of all your skills and they suit us most admirably. We have a job for you. You will be given all the required details and we need you here to take your picture for false passports and identities should they be needed. We'll do that today then once done we'll leave a package for you at the main door. If you could wait until the green light comes on it will all be ready. It should only take a half hour. Please, just sit in the chair over in the corner while it's all being done. You'll find it in a machine. Press seven, forward stroke two, seven, nine, four then it will be deposited in the tray beneath. Thank you for joining us."

As if they had a choice! They did what the voice said then headed for home. They were now an official Assassin. Their conscience would have to shut up!

ALFRED JONES SOON ASSERTED HIMSELF IN PRISON. THE PREvious 'top dog' was demoted and what Big Al said went. He asked for a visit from his Lawyer who duly came and they were put in a room together with a guard waiting outside. The lawyer was in Big Al's pocket and was used to breaking the law for him. How he hadn't been caught was a mystery. Big Al got out a drawing of Robert's face and handed it to the lawyer.

"I want a contract out on this guy. I told him I'd see him dead!"

"I know somebody who can help with that. Have you any cash to cover the fees?"

"My family" - he meant his gang - "have my savings you should be able to get it from them. Ask for Roger."

"Okay" said his lawyer "I know where your family live, I'll see them."

"Bring the contract with you next time you come."

"Yes, I will Al. I know you need this matter sorted out as soon as possible. I'll see you when the contract is ready. It'll need your signature, then it will be enacted." He got up to go and the guard let him out.

"Get up and move, it's back to your cell for you" the guard warned Big Al.

Had he wanted to, Big Al could have flattened the guard irrespective of his size and baton but he wanted this contract on Robert fulfilled. He was a 'model' prisoner for now. Alfred Jones had had good parents who were horrified at what he'd done. He had done well at school but had been the class bully, soon bending terrified kids to his will. He passed all his exams on account of his photographic memory. He never told anyone he had that. They thought he was clever so he basked in their praise. He was also good at sport and played football. He really had no excuse for what he had become. He had chosen a life of crime from a young age. He had spent time in a Juvenile Detention Centre but no-one could persuade him to change his mind, he loved what he did. His lawyer would take care to get the contract on Robert fulfilled. He had been of use to Big Al for some time. He knew if he crossed him Big Al's gang would deal with him. Al went back to his cell feeling satisfied. He had everyone in control.

THE JOHNSONS HAD DULY ACTED ON THE CAPTAIN'S ADVICE. The girls were taking lessons at their local gun club and were getting on well. Things had been quiet for a while but they didn't let that give them a false sense of security. Joanna had told Craig the story from Fraser and warned him to take care too as they were probably watching them all and she didn't want him in harm's way because of her family. She had asked him if he owned a gun.

"No, Jo, I don't but maybe I'd better and join you at the gun club. We see enough of what guns can do. Can't anything more be done by the Police?"

"No, that's the problem until one of us gets hurt their hands are tied."

"That's just great!" said Craig. "I wish I could take you away from all this but we can't, can we? We're not due any free time, at least not a week or so until a month or so's time."

"I know. I'd love to get away. Maybe when the week is due, we can fix it so we're both off. Separate bedrooms though."

He kissed her lightly on the head. He knew what she and her family believed and he respected them. He loved Jo enough to wait. They had talked wedding plans before but the time never seemed right. Now was definitely not the right time.

"We're real stuck at the moment Craig, I'm just so sorry you're caught up in this too." "Don't worry Honey I'll be careful." They got up, held each other tightly and kissed then went back to work.

Meanwhile, across from the hospital a man with a long lens camera was busy scoping them out. He would have enough for Big Al's gang. He now had clear photos of them both which would please the gang. He now needed to wait a while to see which car was Joanna's and get shots of that with the number plate. He knew he had an hour to kill since he had made it his business to find out when she would leave. He'd gone into the hospital and asked when his niece Joanna Johnson left work. "Sure, I can help you with that", said the ward clerk. "Five, Sir".

"Thanks a lot".

"No trouble Sir".

He went into a coffee shop and ordered a cup. "Want anything from the menu Sir?" He looked it over.

"A bowl of chilli please."

"Okay".

She seemed to be quite a perky girl unlike the woman at the far end. Being a photographer, his eyes picked out everything in the room. His chilli arrived and to his surprise was good. He glanced at his watch surprised that after his meal he only had twenty minutes. He put his hand up for the waitress.

"Yes Sir?"

"A refill of coffee please."

She did as he asked and added the cream. He was impressed that she'd remembered that. By the time he'd drunk that it was time to go back into the hospital and wait. Sure enough, just after five Joanna left the building little knowing that she was being tailed. She got in her car and began to leave the hospital. The long lens had been busy again. If anyone asked what he was doing he'd say he was a newspaper reporter trying to get a story. The gang would be pleased with this, very pleased indeed and he'd earned his money. He was well satisfied.

Unknown to him the Security Guard had noticed his actions and reported it through his cell phone. Another Guard came out and they watched the guy as he headed for his car. They started to run in order to intercept him but were too late. He had gone but one of them had got his licence plate number and was relaying it on to the Police.

"See if you can get a match. This guy was acting very suspiciously. We think he was taking pictures of one of the nurses. Do you have any information about any of our nurses being at risk?"

The Police man who had taken the call said, "Hold on, I know we are covering a family at the moment let me see, oh Captain Bedford is here. He's just on his way out but he'll speak to you hold on."

"Captain Bedford here".

He listened intently as the Guard relayed the news and repeated the question. Instantly he thought of the Johnson family. He had the kind of mind that could file cases away and bring one out when needed.

"Yes, we have a family we're doing a drive by at the moment.

The two girls are both nurses. My guess is that he is acting for Big Al's gang to do further damage to the family. You got the licence plate? Hold on while I write it down. Thanks, we'll run that and see what we get. The only snag is it may be a stolen car. We'll see. Give me your name and that of the other Security Guard and we'll get back to you." He jotted them down. "Okay, I've got that. Thanks for your help."

He went back into the office and called the Officers that were there.

"We need to have a team meeting in the morning. Jack, could you text everyone for eight in the morning? Thank you".

He rang Robert's cellphone to warn him that his girls were in danger. "Robert, we still can't do anything until his gang acts but I'll put a plain clothed officer in a car not far from your home during the day. I'm sorry I can't do more but we will be seeking further help. The Feds are going to be brought into this gang situation. This gang especially, Al's one has been active for over a year now. We can't take them all out but Al's is the head of the snake. If we stop his gang, Sebastian's Peak will be a better place to live in. I'll touch base with you after my meeting tomorrow."

"Thanks for the update", said Robert. "I'm very grateful to you". He texted the family then went back to his job.

Captain Bedford had spent most of his young years in England. Therefore he very rarely slipped into American slang unless he was really angry. His parents had brought him to America when he was sixteen. They had wanted to live in Sebastian's Peak, so-named because of the huge lighthouse that stood at the peak of the mountain and used to be manned by a man named Sebastian. Sebastian's Peak had a large beach and plenty of walks for those who were energetic. The rocks were treacherous though, and could not be seen at night. The Light-house was automated now and Sebastian had long gone but it had been a lovely place to grow up in. Everyone looked out for each other. That still held. If anyone had a death the neighbours would be outside the door bringing their casseroles and offering help. It was only in later years that the gangs had taken a real hold over the community. Captain Bedford had seen enough of it and it was escalating. It was time to bring the Feds in and see if together they could sort the crime wave out. Promptly all his officers turned up at eight o'clock in the morning. There was a knock on the door and one of the officers opened it to a plain clothed man outside.

"That'll be Special Agent Jake Hanson of the Fed. Do come in Jake", said Captain Bedford. "Please all grab a seat."

When they were seated he took out a pen and approached the wall where they had a map of America. "Now, we're here in Sebastian's Peak". He circled it. "That's where the Gang is situated somewhere here and it reaches out from this city to the neighbouring towns." He marked out the towns. "You could almost say it's like a spider's web. Jake do you have any input?"

"Yes. Our problem is that on the whole they act under disguise as it were. We never see them in focus until they do something like they're doing now on the orders of Big Al. Otherwise they're silent in their dealings. They don't sell drugs to kids. We know they do to adults but they are very clever, they use a different place each time and act under the radar. People are given a different location each week to get their drugs so we can't keep track of them. The only way is for one of our operatives to infiltrate the gang. I have a man in mind. He's been very useful to us recently. He's currently resting up after exposing a huge money laundering operation but he'll be ready in a week or so to try and take this gang down. He's known as Mitch. We never let him use his real name. We can have his false i.d.'s ready in a week and we think we know where at least one of the gang members lives so he can start there. A guy named Roger seems to be the Deputy when Big Al's not giving the orders. We've had eyes on him for a while. He seems to live at the same house when he's been tailed, so we'll send Mitch there with some made up story that will get him in. The problem is they're a close-knit organisation and convincing them isn't easy. Also, Mitch will be asked to prove himself and sometimes that does mean he has to take a life which is the gruesome part of joining the gang. We hate it, as he does, but it's a necessary evil."

"Is there anything we can do meantime?" asked Captain Bedford.

"Make a Police presence evident. We need a three-pronged attack here, here, and here. He pointed to the map. The family who's being targeted by Al are in a lot of danger. They've had death threats and they especially want the head of the family killed as he gave evidence that got Al incarcerated, but recently Security Guards caught a guy long-lensing one of the girls. He's no doubt been sent there by the gang so they've got her photo and probably licence plate. We ran his but it was a stolen car."

"Okay" said Jake "I'll go and see them. The guy works for the Secret-Service, doesn't he?"

"Yeah".

"So, he'll have some idea of what may come if all else fails?"

"Probably".

"Okay, give me their address and I'll go see them. Okay the rest of you, we have some areas to cover so we need to plan that out. Stay put. Jake, thanks for coming. Appreciate your help."

"That's okay. We'll work together and see what we come up with."

"Sure, appreciate it. Swan, there's a list of all the Sherriffs over in the desk. Could you contact all of them? Tell all of them what we've discussed and ask them to make themselves seen as well. Thanks."

Captain Bedford picked up the phone and dialled Robert's number. He got voice mail and put the phone down, having left a message but ten minutes later Robert rang him back.

"I've got some news for you," said Captain Bedford. "Special Agent Jake Hanson will be calling to see you. I've given him your address and phone number and I had the feeling it would be soon. We're trying to zero in on Al's Gang now. This used to be a lovely part of the city as I'm sure you remember."

"Yes, it was like a suburb rather than a city", said Robert.

"Due to the work you do which is known only to me you know how hard it is to flush these gangs out but we're going to try. Have you upgraded your home by the way?"

"Yes, I have and we're going to have security cameras put in as well."

"Yes, I should have mentioned that, good idea, any more threats?"

"Not at present but we're being vigilant."

"Good, stay that way. One thing, our man who's watching your home in the car said he saw a man in the evening taking a note of your number plates. He finishes at eight, that's how he saw him."

"Thanks for the heads up. I'll tell the family to take extra care."

"Speak to you later Robert when I have more news. 'Bye for now".

The Johnson family were all in at the same time. The girls had done early shifts and spent a little time lying down. Beth brought in the hot-pot she had made and began to ladle it out to each of them. Just as they sat down a spray of bullets were sent ricocheting at their lower window. They had had toughened glass fitted so most of the damage was outside not inside as it could have been.

"Beth, ring the Police. I'll quickly inspect the damage."

The damage wasn't as bad as it could have been, thankfully. He was so grateful they'd had the toughened glass fitted when they moved in.

"It's outside, Beth. We'll need an emergency glazer who can board it up for us tonight. Let's finish our dinner then we can get on to them."

They ate in silence. Unknown to them the man in the car who was observing them had already called it in and was following at a safe distance. There were two men in the car - one driving the other the shooter. There was a squeal of sirens as squad cars moved in from every direction boxing them in. The shooter started to shoot at the squad car nearest him. A gun fight ensued, the officers taking cover as best they could. Some of the other officers in the "box" started out of their cars to shoot. They were like cats advancing cautiously on their prey. Inch by inch they moved. The shooter had to run out of bullets sometime and they really wanted these guys alive if possible. They waited patiently, then, the moment they had been waiting for. The shooter's guns were spent. They still used caution. They approached from the four quadrants and soon had them well and truly covered. An officer took out a megaphone.

"Get out of your car and assume the position. Don't make us kill you."

The driver's door opened tentatively and the guy got out slowly. Then the passenger followed suit. They stood with their hands on the roof of the car. The officers moved in. This was a scoop for them. They would hopefully get some useful information out of them. Captain Bedford would be pleased. It had been a good catch.

The officers read them their rights and transferred them to separate police cars. Once they had arrived at the station, they were put in a holding cell.

"Sarge, we caught them red-handed attacking the Johnsons' property."

"I must admit", said the weary Sargeant "I never thought we'd catch any from Al's gang. Let Captain Bedford know. He may want to take part in the interrogation".

"I'll ring him now Sarge."

Captain Bedford was elated to hear the news. Yes, he would come and view the interrogation. He didn't have far to go. His room was near the top of the Police Station so he only had to get the lift two floors down. He wasn't sure how much they would get out of a couple of teenagers but hey, it was a good day for the Force. In the cell the two boys were feeling the heat of the law.

"What're we gonna to do", asked Tim.

"I dun'now. We cross Big Al, we're in deeper trouble than we are with the Cops."

"I know", said Matt. "I'm trying to think of something to get us out of it but they caught us red-handed so there isn't much we can say, Big Al or not."

"I'm scared" said Tim. "Me too. We've never been caught before."

"Well it's not like we can plead not guilty."

"No, I know". They sat in silence and for the first time in their lives were out of words. After a while Tim broke the silence.

"Dad's gonna be furious."

"Don't you think I know that", shouted Matt. "We could just use the first amendment. We can't do anything now, they're coming for us."

"Oh man". Sure enough, two Officers were approaching their cell.

"Hands behind your backs," said one of the officers. They did what he said and were hand-cuffed as the other officer opened the cell. "Out, the pair of you."

They took them both to separate interview rooms. Now Tim was really scared. He'd thought they would be held together. He relied on Matt to know what to do. Soon, one of the officers entered Tim's room whilst another entered Matt's room.

"Do they have any 'priors'?" asked Captain Bedford.

"No" replied the Sergeant.

"One wonders why they get mixed up in crime. Matt's only seventeen and Tim is sixteen. Is it parenting or just their own free will? Who knows? I sincerely hope we can get some useful information out of them."

"We have a shot at the interview now," said the Sargeant.

"Right let's see how they try to get out of this one."

The officer sat down opposite Matt. He shuffled some papers. "Let's see, Matt Muller you've never been in trouble before. Or was that because we didn't catch the two of you before? You're in a jam now and I can help you if you help me. That seem fair?"

Matt sat in silence.

"So, what's it to be?"

"I don't know what to say."

"Tell me how you got into Big Al's gang for a start." Matt had been sitting with his arms folded in defensive mode. Now he put both hands on the desk.

"Can I have a drink?"

"Sure. Hold on." He opened the door and shouted "Can somebody get some water and a coffee please?"

He knew they were being watched but he didn't want the kid to know. Soon a bottle of water arrived and a hot coffee. Matt drank half the bottle.

"Okay Matt you've drunk your water, now are you going to help me so I can help you? You've got no defence, we caught you red-handed. How'd you get into Al's gang?"

Matt crumbled, he knew there was no way out now.

"His men trained us when we were nine and ten. It was

robbing at first. Then we went up to shop robbing with a fake gun that looked real."

"Who got you in, in the first place?"

"A guy named Roger. He told us he'd been looking for young guys like us and would we like to join him. When we saw the money they were offering we were more than interested."

"How much did they offer you?"

"Forty dollars at first then when we did the shop robbing it went up to sixty."

"Was that each or split between you?"

"Each, we'd got about eight hundred dollars with the shop robbing. They were very pleased with us."

"I'm sure they were. Do you know where Roger lives?"

"I'm going to need protection for me and my brother if I tell you. Can you help keep us safe? Al's gang are everywhere and we're scared."

"Like I said, you help us we help you. We can make you disappear if need be." "What d'you mean?"

"You ever heard of the witness protection plan?"

"No. What's that?"

"We take you and your family and move you to a new place to live and we give you false i.d.'s so you start over fresh in a new place but you have to keep out of crime. We'll put that to the Judge when you go to court."

"Okay, he lives on nine six four Blackwood Street."

"Thank you, Matt. Your parents are here and have heard everything you've said." "They'll kill us."

"I don't think so. Let me take you out, but could you please sign this statement?"

Matt scribbled his signature. "Thank you. Now follow me.

We'll go get your brother and take you to your parents. We need to take your photos and fingerprints. Come this way."

He led Matt up a corridor where Tim was being held. Tim came out looking scared. "What did you tell them man?"

"All of it" said Matt. "What did you say?"

"Some of it. We got no way out Matt except to let them help us, have we?"

"No Tim. We got to start off fresh and stop the robbing. They got us for the shooting. We'll be tried in an Adult court. Good job we never killed nobody or we'd be in jail for sure."

"I'm scared Matt. What if we go to prison? Al will get at us somehow."

"I know, but the officers say we should disappear after the information I gave them. I think we have a chance."

"I sure hope you're right. Oh boy here's Mom and Dad."

Their parents approached them. Their Dad spoke first. "Why ever didn't you tell us when all this started? We could have helped you."

"Yeah, like you'd have listened. You're both always too busy to listen to us, that's why we joined the gang. They were like a family," said Matt.

"As mad as I am with you son you do have a point, we've not been there for you."

Their Mother began to cry. "What you both have done is awful but I never should have gone back to work. It's not like we need the money. I should've stayed home for you two. Don't get me wrong, you made a choice that you knew was wrong. We taught you right from wrong you made a real bad choice. I just hope the Judge will go for what the officer offered."

"Yeah", said their Dad. "You're in deep trouble now. I'm sorry we failed you."

The officer approached them. "We are going to move you to a safe house until the trial is over. Go home, get what you all want from your home, just the basics please. Things that matter to you are okay but don't make your cases too heavy. You tell your neighbours you have to go away for a while and would they please keep an eye on the house. Then you get a taxi back here. We'll get you one to your home. We don't want Police cars in the picture."

"Thank you", said the boys' Dad. "We're very grateful for all your help."

"We see this every day", said the officer. "Kids choose their own path no matter how well they're brought up. I think your wife was very brave acknowledging it was because she hadn't been there for them. Most parents of your class don't and the ones who get into it because their parents ill treat them and don't give a damn. We have enough information to try and get some of Al's gang now. Roger is quite high up; we think the Deputy, so if we can get him it will a good catch. I'm going to order your cab now". He went off and entered a room that must have been his office.

The boys sat in silence. Their Dad said "How long have you been in the gang?" "Since we were ten and nine Dad."

"Oh my", said their Dad.

Their Mom began to cry again. "To think we didn't notice something", she said through her tears. "It's like a bad dream".

"Yeah" said their Dad. "I feel so angry at you but there's no going back and you've been caught today. You realise you could've killed someone."

"I know Dad", said Matt. Tim had been silent but then spoke up "We're sorry Mom and Dad we just got in too deep. We had to prove ourselves to the gang. The next step would've been killing."

Their parents were in a state of shock. "Oh man", said their Dad "What were you thinking!"

"We didn't Dad. We tried not to think of that part. We wanted out but they had us tied in so deep we couldn't get out. They'd have killed us".

The officers had arranged someone to get them some drinks. She came over to ask what they wanted. She saw the parents were both white with the shock of it and asked the resident Counsellor to come over which he did.

"Hi, I'm the Police's Counsellor here. Can I be of help? Ann, get them some tea or coffee?"

Their parents asked for coffee and the boys juice. Ann went off to get them. "My name is Richard. I can see your parents are in a state of shock boys so I'll ask you both if there is anything you want to say. It's best to get it out."

Their Dad said "I'm angry but can see where we went wrong. We were never there for them. Even when they had special events at school that they were in we were too busy. Our maid was more of a parent to them than us. It's chilling to think that the next step would be them having to kill someone."

Richard said "It's good that you can see it like that. I see lots of parents in here who are always working and won't take any of the blame. I think you're all going to be okay". Ann walked over and said "Their taxi's here." "Okay", said Richard. "Good meeting you."

They got into the cab feeling drained. Their sons were silent then Matt said "We're really sorry aren't we Tim?" "Yeah we are".

Captain Bedford was delighted. "Finally, we have an address, a place to start. We need to get started as fast as possible now. Richard, call all the Officers and get them ready to roll. I'll call the Feds and see if they want in too." He picked up the phone and dialled Jake's number. "Jake we've finally got a lead on Roger. We're gearing up to launch a sting operation. You want in?"

"Sure do. When are you going to move?"

"The guys have to get their gear on then we're good to go." He gave Jake the address. "Okay. Meet you there".

They were all used to moving fast and were ready to go. The cars moved to their locations knowing they had to box the gang in. Captain Bedford took out a megaphone. "This is the Police. Come out with your hands up and you won't get shot." A bullet was his answer. "Okay everyone, move in NOW!" They moved cautiously in on the location. Gun fire now was on both sides as the Gang tried to defend their territory. The snipers were ready should anyone come out shooting. A prolonged battle ensued. Finally, the gang seemed to run out of ammunition. Everyone was on guard knowing it could be a ruse. Then the door opened and a couple of men came out. They each threw a lit up bottle containing a stick of dynamite at the nearest Police cars. The Officers moved quickly out of their cars and sped away, falling to the ground, knowing the cars would explode which they soon did.

Captain Bedford picked up his car radio. "Bring the helicopter in." The battle was heating up now. The hope was that the helicopter could attack them from different angles and speed up the fight. "They must have an arsenal in there," said Captain Bedford to Jake who was sitting beside him."

"Yeah sure seems like it. We need them to run out. Soon would be good."

"Agreed. Ah what do we have here?" Three men stepped out with their hands up. The Police radio sounded. Captain Bedford picked it up. "They're coming out the back Sir with their hands up." "Move in everybody."

They moved cautiously stalking their prey, ever vigilant, wary of traps. The officers were cuffing them as they moved out and loading them into Police vans. There were twelve in all living in the house. It was all over. They had got their prey. Now would come the task of identifying Roger. They were speedily moved down to the Police station and put in holding cells. When Captain Bedford got back the boys had come back with their parents. This would really help. They knew Roger and could identify him for them. They had to come up before the DA and a Judge during the time they were in the safe house. It would be a long night for them.

"Richard, get the men in a lineup would you? I'll go fill the boys in," said Captain Bedford. He went to see the boys. Their parents looked weary and still in a state of shock. The Captain told the boys how the one-way mirror worked and that they would be safe through-out. Matt said he would do it. Their parents looked alarmed. "Don't worry, they won't see Matt entering or leaving if that's what's troubling you. We get the men in first then take them out first so Matt is the last to go in and come out. At no time do we allow our people to be identified."

Matt entered the room. He looked them all over carefully. "He's not here. The others just carried out his orders."

This was not what the Captain wanted to hear. Roger had got

away and most likely had another branch of the gang he could go to and hide out, whilst still giving the orders. This was a bitter blow and made it even more vital that they get the boys relocated.

"Thank you for your help Matt, it's just a shame we didn't get Roger this time."

"They know how to re-locate fast Sir" said Matt. "They have loads of houses all over the city." This was worrying.

"Any other places you been at?"

"No Sir just that one but Tim and I heard them talking about location A, B and C and so on. Never a name or number."

"Never mind. We've got twelve to interrogate so that's going to keep us busy. My men will take you all to the safe house tonight but you know that's not the end of it for you. Charges will be brought against the pair of you."

Their Mother began to cry again. "Don't Mom" said Tim who had remained silent for some time. "We knew we were doing wrong. We just chose to do it. When we did the drive-by shooting it was me that did the firing. It was like a drug, the more we did things the more of a rush we got."

"Yeah" said Matt. "we're really sorry."

"Sorry won't cut it this time son" said their father. "You have to pay now you've been caught. Thank God you didn't kill anyone tonight. We know we've not been the best parents so we take some of the blame but we taught you right from wrong. You chose to do wrong. I'm very disappointed in you both."

The boys hung their heads in shame. An officer approached them. "We need a sketch of Roger. Could you boys come and help us with that please? Sorry to keep you waiting around Mr and Mrs Kent but we need to do this then get the boys processed. We've not got a photo of them both or their fingerprints yet.

I'll get someone to get you a coffee. Would you like to see the Counsellor again?"

"No thanks but the coffee would be good thank you."

"Okay I'll send some over. Boys follow me please." They were led inside an office where a man was waiting with his pencil at the ready.

"Sit down boys. I'm Ted. First we're going to start with you giving me a face shape and so on." Pretty soon they had a rough sketch of Roger. The boys continued adding bits to it and before long they had a likeness. That would help the Police greatly. Ted picked up his phone and began to dial.

"I'm finished with the boys here. Okay I'll bring them over. Follow me please." They were led into a room where a camera could be seen.

An Officer came in. "Right boys here are your number plates. Stand over there please and hold the plate up. Matt went first then Tim. "Now fingerprinting comes next." They had that done then were returned to their parents.

07

Back at the Johnson house the neighbours had all come out following the drive-by shooting. Police cars were there and the Police were taking any statements any of them could offer. One neighbour, Olivia, said she could remember the number plate as the car sped away. It was taken down along with any other offerings, which weren't much. One of the officers was inside with the family.

"We caught the men who did it. They're just teenagers who made the wrong choice. They have no priors. Do you want to prosecute them?" It sounded like the stupidest statement anyone could make. "I ask because we are taking them to a safe house as Al's Deputy, Roger, has not been caught and he knows the boys will rat on him to save their own skins."

"Well what do you expect us to say, that we're sorry for them?" exploded Robert. "Of course we do!"

"I can understand that I'd feel the same myself. Okay I'll write that up. There is a chance that they will have to go into the witness protection plan as Roger will have them killed."

"This just gets better and better" shouted Robert. "We're the ones that need protecting not outlaws! They are lucky none of us got a fatal bullet this evening or they'd be looking at a long sentence, maybe even the death sentence!"

"Robert, sit down and have a coffee", said Beth. Robert sat down shaking with rage. "Easy, Honey, easy". She was always the voice of reason in a storm. Everyone was shaken up.

A man approached the house. "I'm the glazier. When can I board this up?"

"We're pretty much done with it. You can start now" said the officer at the door. "Good, I'll get my tools."

The family would be notified should Roger have been caught. It would give them some solace. Back in the house the officer there had taken all their statements and there was nothing left for him to do. The Police left and the glazier took their place. The hotpot that Beth had prepared was unsalvageable. None of them felt like eating but they knew they should, so Beth got up to make some sandwiches. There was a ring on the doorbell. Outside, were a group of ladies with casseroles in their hands. Celia led the group. "We know you won't feel like cooking tonight so here's some for you, one for tonight the rest for the freezer when they've cooled down."

Beth dissolved into tears at the kindness. Evil may have come to this city but the old, good neighbourly ways were not forgotten. "Please, come in all of you. We were just about to have sandwiches thank you all so much."

"You just sit Beth Honey and let us do the rest." Soon the women were busy in the kitchen clearing up the ruined hot pot and disposing of it. Loading the dishwasher and lining up the casseroles for the freezer later. Fresh plates were got out and laid on the table and a hot casserole was placed in the middle. Fresh coffee was on the boil and once all was done, they were all hugged and the neighbours left with Celia saying: "Now don't you let that food get cold none. You enjoy it now you hear".

They all looked at each other then went to the table and dived in, not realising how hungry they were. "Good always triumphs over evil. We've just seen that" said a red-eyed Beth. "This is good and we'll feel better for the meal."

"Yes, I feel better now" said Robert. The girls picked up the empty plates and loaded them in the dishwasher. It was full so they turned it on. "I'm so glad you were on early shifts girls or you may have been hit by a stray bullet. The Police found bullets near the cars" said Beth. "We have a lot to be grateful for."

"Yes". Said Robert, I've calmed down a bit now but how criminals can get special treatment is beyond me."

Josephine spoke up. "I'm a bit worried about going out tonight with Alex. She had met him some months ago. "I think just for tonight it may be good to stay in."

"But you can't let them rule your lives. That's what they want - to terrorise us," said Robert.

The girls rang their boy-friends and told them what had happened and just for tonight they were staying in. The doorbell rang. It was a reporter from Channel CCGN.

"Can we get a statement from you about what happened here?"

"I just want the people who are terrorising us to know that we're not going to let them win. The day will come when they are in prison where they deserve to be," said Robert.

"Do you have anything else to say? You could have been killed," said the Reporter. "Yes, we know that but by the grace of God we weren't. I have nothing else to say" said Robert, beginning to close the door.

The reporter was speaking to the camera. "Well there you have it. A brave family…"

Half an hour later the glazier rang the bell. "You're all done. I've boarded you to the top as the glass literally just broke so you're well covered. You may want to consider bulletproof glass. Here's an estimate for ordinary glass and the bulletproof. As you can see, I can give you a good deal on it but you're well protected at the moment. The boards are stronger than glass so you'll be safe. Let me know your decision when you're ready. Good night Sir." Robert thanked him then closed the door.

An hour later the phone rang and it was Captain Bedford. "How are you all holding up? An officer filled you in I know but I'd like to come and see you when the time is right for you, would that be okay?"

"Yes," said Robert. That would be good. We're holding it together but we're well shaken up."

"Right we'll arrange something at a later date. I'll let you recover for now."

"Thank you, I'll get back to you." He put down the phone. "That was Captain Bedford. He wants to see us when it's a good time for us. Right now, we need some recovery time."

The girls came down from their bedrooms having told their boy-friends the situation. "We're out tomorrow night instead," said Joanna.

"Okay girls," said Beth. "We'll try and have a relaxing evening then. Let's put a film on, shall we?" They all agreed and let the movie take them away from the reality of what had happened.

When Robert went to work the next day, his Boss asked him to come to his office. "I saw the news last night and heard what happened. I have to tell you that from what Dave has been able to uncover on the terrorists it sounds like Big Al has a contract out on you, a trained Assassin. We don't know where they are at the moment but it seems they have a way to go to get to you yet, but I wanted you to know so you can tell the Police."

"Oh boy," said Robert. "It just gets better and better. It's like a nightmare."

"Yeah, it is Robert. We'll keep you updated and I'll call the Police if you like. From information we have, Roger is controlling everything in Al's gang. It's a pity he escaped but we're on this Rob, we're with you."

"Thank you, I appreciate that."

"Now, do you want to stay working or take the day off? News like that is hard to take. I don't know how I'd feel."

"No, I'll stay working to get my mind off it."

"Fair enough. I'll ring the Police for you."

"Thanks, I really don't want to talk to them at the moment."

Robert left the office and made his way to his desk. This was chilling news. Should he share it with Beth or keep it to himself? He didn't know what to do. How their lives had changed since he gave his testimony. He felt guilty for putting his family at risk. He tried to concentrate on work.

The door opened. His Boss came in. "I've spoken to the Police and Captain Bedford would like to see you on your own. I suggest you go this afternoon."

"Okay thank you I will." As Robert made his way to his car, he wondered what news he would get now. He drove to the Police station and parked his car. Once inside, he was ushered into the Captain's office.

"Robert, thank you for coming. I have a task for you. We know we have a dirty cop as someone is leaking out information. I have a list here of all our officers including their bank account numbers. I want you to hack in to their computers and see if any large transactions of money have been put into any of their accounts. Would you do that for me please?"

"Yes sure. It'll take a while to hack in to all of them but I'll get on it. You've heard my latest news."

"Yes, we hope to intercept them. We've heard roughly where they are so don't give up."

"I feel drained to be honest. I did the right thing and all of us are at risk."

"I can only imagine what you're going through. We intend to find Roger but until we can stop this leak we can't act. I've included mine in there so you know I'm clean. This gang will be taken down, we intend to keep the people safe. Thanks for helping."

"It helps to do something but I'm real sorry to hear you have a leak."

"Yes, it leaves a bad taste. Go home Robert and try to relax if you can."

"Thanks, I will. I'll get on to this tomorrow."

"Okay." They shook hands and Robert left. Driving home, he thought: "So that's how Roger got away. A dirty cop." He got home and saw Josephine's car there. He put the coffee pot on. Beth would be home in a couple of hours. Footsteps on the stairs alerted him to Josephine coming down them.

"Dad, what are you doing home?"

"I had to see Captain Bedford then my Boss told me to come home."

"What did he want?"

Oh boy, what should he tell her? "I have to do a job for him." Don't ask anymore please don't, he thought.

"Okay."

"Want a coffee, Jo, I've put the machine on?"

"That would be good. We had one heck of a morning. I literally was holding one guy's heart in my hands until we got him to surgery."

Robert poured the coffee in silence and handed one to Jo. "That takes dedication Jo. I'm proud of you."

"We get so many gunshot wounds and even kids are shooting kids. It's pretty awful." "Sounds it Jo. I don't know how you do it."

"I love my job even with all that. I feel I'm making a difference. I guess you feel that, working for the Government."

"Yes, I do." He knew he would have to tell the family about the Assassin but he would wait until they were all home and after they'd had their meal.

The family had all eaten and Robert wondered how they would take the news. "I have to tell you all something," he began. "It's not good news. I learned today that Al has a contract out on me, an Assassin. The Police are on it and hope to stop them so I have to be on my guard. We still have a plain-clothed policeman watching the house but we're not covered at night. I've been thinking about that and an old friend of mine who has post-traumatic stress disorder can't sleep at night. He served in Iraq and Syria so he has bad dreams. I'm thinking of asking him to come take care of us at night. What do you think? He's a lovely guy very protective and good at what he does. We'll give him the guest room for when he wants to sleep during the day and pay him of course."

"I think that's a good idea," said Beth. "It would make us all sleep a bit better."

"Yes," echoed the girls.

"I'll do that then," said Robert. "He's a good man and I trust him literally with my life."

Beth was in shock at the news about her husband being a target for someone to shoot. She started shaking. The girls immediately knew what to do and ministered to her. "Dad, get her a coffee please." Robert did as he was asked. "Take a sip Mom," said Joanna, "It'll help".

Slowly Beth began to recover. Robert hugged her. "I know it's scary news. I admit I'm scared but we can't let Al win. This is what he wants, for us to live in terror."

"I know Robert but I don't want to lose you."

Robert held her tight and said "I've got people working on finding them so they may get caught before they even get here if that helps you to know."

"Yes, Robert it does. I feel a bit better now thank you. I'll have that coffee now."

Robert let go of her so she could drink. "Girls, are you okay?" "It's a shock Dad" said Joanna. "We see awful things all the time but nothing prepares you for the shock especially when it's you."

"Yes," said Josephine, "I feel the same. Do you think Sam could be your personal bodyguard and watch you by day as well?"

"Josephine, when do you think the poor guy's going to get some sleep?"

"Oh, I didn't think of that but you could do with a bodyguard."

"Yes, that's a good idea," said Beth, "but how would we find one?"

"I'll ask Captain Bedford," said Robert, "it's a good idea. First, I'll go see Sam and see if he can help us. I'll give the Captain a ring in a minute. He knew that the news would be a shock and told me to give him a ring. I've got his home number. I'll mention the bodyguard thing and see what he says." He got up and went to the hall phone so the family could continue coming to terms with it in the living room. He dialled the number. Captain Bedford answered. "Ah, Robert, how did they take it?"

"Well enough but they're shaken up. My daughter came up with the idea of a bodyguard, I don't know how do-able that is?"

"I know someone who used to be one but he's retired now. I could ask him if he knows someone."

"Thank you, that would give my family a great deal of relief."

"I'd send one of the officers but until that matter that we spoke about has been done I can't do it."

"Thanks, I appreciate the thought but I know the position you're in but if you could have a word with the guy you know that would help ease my family's minds and mine, I have to say."

"I'll see what I can do tomorrow and get back to you when I have any news."

"Thank you, I really appreciate that."

"Okay, try and get some sleep, I'll get back to you, 'bye." Robert echoed the same and put the phone down. He went back to the living room. His family looked at him hopefully.

"He said he knows a guy who used to do it but is retired. He may know someone though so he's going to get in touch with him."

"Thank God," said Beth, "at last something positive. Girls, are you on an early or a late?"

"I'm on an early said Josephine."

"I'm on a late," said Joanna, "why Dad?"

"Be on your guard when you're driving. They've got all our number plates."

"We will Dad."

"Just be over cautious now that we know someone's after me. Heaven knows what they'll do." He had horrid visions of one of them being held hostage. "And I think you should keep the guns we bought you with you."

"Aw heck Dad isn't that going a bit far?"

"No, I don't think so. This Assassin is capable of doing anything to get to me. I'm afraid for you."

"I hadn't thought of it that way," said Joanna. "We'll do that if it makes you feel better."

"Beth, have you got yours with you?"

"Yes, I have Robert. Ever since the school-shooting I've had it with me."

"Good, we've done all we can tonight. Let's see what tomorrow brings." Beth wearily made her way up the stairs followed by Robert. The girls stayed up to watch a movie.

The following day Robert got to work on the information the Captain had given him. He would have to be careful and not leave a trace of his hacking. It would take him some time but his Boss had given him the heads up. Doing that at least took his mind off of family problems at the moment. He would look up Sam tomorrow being Saturday and see what he could arrange.

08

The Assassin didn't feel right. They were having difficulty breathing and their chest felt tight. They rang the buzzer for the Hostess. She wasn't long coming - this was first class after all. "Yes, how can I help?"

"Doctor" croaked the Assassin. The Hostess could see this was an emergency and got the Doctor straight away. He listened to the Assassin's chest and said: "You've got bronchitis but a really bad case. It's hospital for you when we de-plane. There's a hospital there called 'Hope Hospital.' They'll look after you well. I have some anti-biotics in my bag. Are you allergic to anything?"

"No."

"Right let's get you started on these. They'll help for now but I think you will need stronger ones to stop it getting worse. I don't want to alarm you but you are very ill. I'll take your temperature. Yes, as I thought, high - so you need some Tylenol for that."

The Assassin was too ill to care about what was happening. They knew they had an emergency number in their passport which the Hospital could ring and let the 'A.A.' know what was happening and they would pick up the bill. They had at least made provision for illness and as long as they were told, the job still went to them when they were better. The Doctor listened to their lungs.

"Yes, very congested. Take these."

He gave them the anti-biotic and the Tylenol. They had a hard time swallowing but got them down. Visions of being in hospital were not welcome. They only had an Army duffle bag and a brief case with them. Some clothing was in the duffle bag and all the lists of informants were in the laptop, plus the plastic gun was in the brief case along with some money. They would want that put in the hospital safe. They had hidden pockets in their jacket where they kept the keys. They felt awful.

"Let's make you more comfortable," said the Doctor. "Mary-Ann, could you please get the patient in bed mode."

"Sure," said Mary-Ann. "Let's get the bed down and get you in it. I'll have to remove your jacket but I'll put it on the shelf with your luggage."

She removed the jacket and did that then she and the Doctor got the Assassin in bed. It came with first class, given business-men often slept on the plane.

"We'll de-plane in an hour", said the Doctor." "I'll make you a priority case so we'll get you into Hospital fast. I'm just going to alert the Airport so we have an ambulance ready."

He did so. Mary-Ann did her best to keep the Assassin comfortable until they de-planed. The ambulance was ready. Two paramedics boarded the plane with a stretcher and whisked them off to the ambulance. The Doctor explained their condition to them and mentioned it could be pneumonia. One of them was taking notes while the other was looking after the Assassin. They'd heard the word pneumonia and knew what that meant. It could be a killer. After all the paperwork was filled in the ambulance started moving.

"We don't have far to go," said the paramedic reassuringly, holding the Assassin's hand as they travelled. The siren was on. They weaved in and out of traffic. Soon they were there and a Doctor came to examine the Assassin again.

"You have pneumonia," he said. "We're taking you up to ICU now."

"Case and jacket," croaked the Assassin "in safe."

"Don't worry, we'll do that and put your duffle bag in storage with your name on it." "Thank you," rasped the Assassin. Good, no-one would know what was in them.

"Try not to talk," said the Doctor "You're very ill. We'll get you started on some stronger anti-biotics and your temperature is very high, we'll keep on top of that, all you need do is let us do our jobs and rest. Be a good patient and it is easier for everyone."

"In passport...emergency number...you must ring that quickly. They need to know I'm ill and will pay bill" croaked the Assassin.

"All right, we'll do that. It seems you were on important business were you? Don't speak just nod. Okay. You don't look the office type so I don't know what line of business you're in but that doesn't matter. We'll do as you ask. No, don't speak again. I gather you were going to thank me?" The Assassin nodded. "Take it as a given. Now, here we are just in this lift and you'll be in ICU. I've written up a 'script for you so they'll do that. Here's an orderly. Take this patient up to ICU please."

The Assassin felt themselves going up in the lift, then the doors parted and they were in ICU. A nurse dressed in scrubs indicated the bed the Assassin should be put on. They felt better when they were in it. They wondered how they had got it, then remembered a man on their first plane had been coughing and spluttering in First Class and a doctor had had to be got for him. The recycled air in the plane did nothing to stop the spread of illness. Now they would have to rest and do what the Doctor had said.

They were drowsy and were just falling into sleep when a nurse came up to them and said: "I have to put some fluids up for you on this stand. You won't want food at the moment but we must keep you hydrated. Now, what's the time? Ten after nine. I'll give you all your drugs now. I will be here with you for the rest of the day, then a night shift nurse will take over from me and watch you all night. That's it, swallow them slowly. They'll help. The Doctor will have told you how ill you are. I'm going to put you on this monitor as well. We'll change your clothing for a gown. No, don't try to help too much. I've got you. There. Not as bad as you thought eh?"

The Assassin really didn't care by then. The Nurse spoke again. "I'm Tracey, one of the night nurses. We come on at nine then the day shift will look after you from seven a.m. We'll be monitoring you all night so I apologise if we wake you but you are seriously ill. A doctor will be in and out checking on you too. The Emergency Doctor told me to tell you that the Hospital has been in touch with your Agency and they have told us to tell you not to worry, just get better. No, don't speak, I can see you trying to. You're in room 27. We've put your bag with your clothing in the wardrobe, the other items are in the safe as you requested. Feel better now?" They nodded. "Good, now I want you to get some rest. Let me just take your blood pressure first. Yes, quite high. Get some rest while you can. I'll be sitting here watching you. In a while you may be so sleepy you don't care. I've seen that happen to patients as ill as you. Right, I think that's everything, you can rest now." She gave the Assassin a reassuring pat on the arm.

The nurse was not joking about them being in and out. It seemed like forever to the Assassin who was on oxygen so couldn't speak. To be honest they didn't even just want to try. It was the first time they had been really ill since having the normal child-hood illnesses. They were fit and hadn't had a cold in years. It was a battle for them to even breathe. More fluids were put up and the Doctor looked concerned at their chart.

"We may have to put the patient onto a vent," he said. "It's a machine that does the breathing for you." The Assassin tried to protest. "No, don't try to argue. Note I said "may." You're very fit, that's in your favour so it may not come to that. Is the oxygen enough for you? Don't try to lie, I'll know." They nodded. "Well we'll give you another hour, if there's no improvement in your breathing we do as I said. Deal?" They nodded agreement. "Right. Nurse what are the other readings, oh, on this other page. Your blood pressure is high and we need to get this down. I don't like the look of this reading. We need to add a beta-blocker that should bring it down." He told the nurse what dose to give. She complied. "This'll take a while to work but it works well. You should have a lower reading in the morning. You may also have cold hands but not many people get it with this. I'm just telling you so you don't worry. That's the last thing I want you to do. Just rest."

As if they could, but they knew that the staff only had their best interests at heart so they had to comply. Horrible visions of past kills flooded their thoughts as they tried to rest. The first kill had been the worst. They had made sure it was a kill shot to the head, so he wouldn't suffer, but the Assassin's hands were shaking afterwards and they felt bile coming up the back of their throat. Pictures of their parents also came to mind, shaking their heads sadly at what their child had become. They were in and out of consciousness all night. A thermometer was put in their ear, a blood pressure cuff was put on their arm and a small peg-like thing was put on her finger. This went on every hour. The Doctor came back half way through the night.

"Well, you're holding your own with the oxygen. That's good news. You won't need assisted help, but you're not out of the woods yet. The night time is the worst though so don't worry, you're doing better than I expected but you're young and fit so that will speed your recovery. We are still going to monitor you every hour though so you won't get much sleep. Let's listen to your chest again. Nurse, help me with this gown." The Nurse did so. "Yes, very congested but I can hear the oxygen's working. Okay, I'll let you rest as best you can."

The Assassin was left with their nightmares for the night.

09

ROBERT HAD SOUGHT OUT SAM AS HE PROMISED ON SATURDAY. He found the address and exited his car. He mounted the stairs and rang the doorbell. Sam answered the door. Once inside, Robert could see that it was a small apartment, neat and tidy and his pal Sam looked as he remembered him.

"How are you Sam?"

"Well enough, thanks Buddy. You've looked me up for a reason, I can tell. What gives?"

"I'm sorry Sam I should have looked you up before. I gave evidence against Big Al who runs a tight-knit gang you may have heard of?"

"Yeah, I've heard of them."

"Well since then he's been terrorising us, and to put it bluntly I need a bodyguard. Do you know anyone? I was thinking of asking you but I know you're still recovering and I don't want to put you in the line of fire again."

"Well I appreciate that but I've made a good recovery. What would it involve?"

"Well, I need someone with me in the morning when I go to work and someone to stay in the house overnight and keep an eye out. We have a plainclothed policeman watching the house all day for any movement but the attacks are usually at night."

"Makes sense. They use the cover of darkness to hide themselves."

"But some of the attacks have been at supper time in broad daylight. They seem to think they're above the law, but when we had a drive-by shooting they caught them. They were just teenagers."

"So, what would you want done at night?"

"Basically, an eye kept out while we sleep. We have a built-in annexe as a guest room upstairs with its own loo and shower. Whoever does this will get the chance to sleep during the day. My girls are nurses so they come home to sleep during the day as well."

"How would you be taken to work with only one car?"

"Oh, I hadn't thought of that. Well, just the night thing then."

"I can do that for you. I don't sleep much at night - the old visions keep coming. I sleep better during the day so that would suit me fine."

"I would really appreciate that Sam just until this thing is over. I'll pay you."

"Aw put your money away man."

Robert didn't know how to thank him. "I insist on giving you something."

"We'll see when it's over."

"Thank you, Sam, I don't know how to thank you."

"Well I'll be getting home cooked meals and I assume your wife will leave me a cold lunch?"

"Oh yes that's right."

"Well you've got yourself a deal Robert. I'll need to know where you're at."

"I have the address here." Robert fished a piece of paper from his pocket. He knew Sam would look after them well and they'd all sleep better knowing someone was on guard. "How are you otherwise Sam? Have you made a full recovery?"

"As best as can be expected they tell me. I'll be glad to have something to do. I get stir crazy. Most of my pals have been killed and the couple that are left I keep in touch with on Skype. Works well. I'll start tomorrow if that's okay with you."

"Yes, wonderful thank you so much Buddy I really appreciate that. We have a double garage so we'll get one of our cars out and you can put your car in there."

"Okay that's fine. I'll see you tomorrow." They shook hands and Robert got up. They had a "man" hug and Robert left. He felt a weight had been lifted off of his shoulders. Once home he told the family the good news. "I'll have to let Captain Bedford know as he'll need to tell the man outside. I'd best do that now." He dialled the number. The Captain wasn't there but an officer promised to ring the plainclothed man straight away so that was covered. "You'll like Sam," he told the family. "I should've seen him before all this. Bad of me, but I'm grateful he's so forgiving. He's happy about the set-up until all this is over."

"Did you tell him an Assassin was after you?" asked Beth.

"No, I'll tell him tomorrow."

The next day, Sam moved in. The family all took to him immediately. He was a lovely guy and easy to get along with.

Beth could see that this was going to work out beautifully. He'd brought his night vision binoculars with him and a night vision telescope with a camera on it that could be used day or night, as could the rest of his equipment. Beth had cooked a roast dinner and Sam was delighted.

"You sure can cook, Mrs Johnson, this is real good."

"Beth, please, and thank you for the compliment."

"Yes," said Robert, "please feel free to call us by our first names."

"Well, Mr Johnson if you're sure. I feel like I'm doing a job for you and I should be formal."

"No, not at all," said Robert. "You're going to become part of the family while you're here. Call me Robert and the girls Joanna and Josephine."

"Well, thank you," said Sam, "if I keep getting food like this I'll be in heaven!"

Beth laughed, delighted. "Let me get you some coffee while you eat your pie. Do you want cream on it?"

"Now you're really spoiling me."

"Not at all. I hope you will feel relaxed among us as we all get to know each other." "Yes," said Robert. "Make yourself at home. I'll show you where the guest room is when we've all finished dinner. You'll be comfortable there."

They finished their meal and coffee and after a while Robert offered to show Sam where the guest room was. It was an enclosed flat with all the mod-cons and an upper room in which there was an exercise bike, desk and chair.

"Good," said Sam, "I was going to ask you if there was a high point in the house. This looks good, I can see over the road and around the house easily as you have one window overlooking the road and the other the side of the house. I'll bunk down here fine. It's a lovely guest room. I'll set up my gear soon."

"I'm glad you have all you need," said Robert. "Beth will do your laundry for you. Just put it in the bin down-stairs."

"Well, said Sam, "I reckon I have a good deal here. You sure know how to make a person feel comfortable. I'll set up my stuff and keep an eye out. Where's the guy in the car?"

Robert pointed him out to him. "Has he been told about me?"

"Yes, I asked an officer to tell him."

"Perfect, are the gang aware of him do you think?"

"It's possible but I believe they've changed the man and the car so they may not catch on. He's in a different position too. I'll show you. He's in that black car over there." Robert pointed to the man who was about four houses away.

"Yeah, I got eyes on him," said Sam. "You got another chair I can put on the other window in here?"

"Yeah sure, I'll get you one down from the attic."

"That'll be fine."

"Don't worry, they are a comfortable chair to sit on."

Sam laughed, remembering some of the fox-holes he had been in in the Army. "Well, I can get used to that," he said.

The house was large, a white painted brick with five bedrooms, all with en-suites. The hall-way had two doors that gave way to the living room. One was a side door and the other was just behind where the large sofa stood, in essence, a back entrance. The living room featured an open fireplace where they burned wood on special occasions like Thanksgiving and Christmas. It was a large room which gave way to the stairs leading to the bedrooms. The attic was a walk-in attic so it made it simple for Robert to get another chair out for Sam. He took it to him.

"That's just fine," said Sam who was feeling a bit overwhelmed by the kindness shown him by this family. Sam was remembering his own family. His Dad had served in the Army and his Mom had worked in an office. He had another brother, Joshua, who had been killed in Iraq. They were a hard-working family and had a nice two-tier house that had served them well. Both his parents were living in a senior citizens' retirement village, where all their needs were met and they had a room for socialising and holding special events. Sam visited them as often as he could and had explained to them that he now had a job, looking after a terrorised family. They were concerned for him naturally, but Sam had explained the matter carefully, knowing they did not want to lose another son.

"You'll get paid for this son?" his Dad had asked.

"Yeah, they've offered but this guy is an old friend."

"You take their money son if they're offering, old friend or not, you're doing a job."

"I guess you're right. I will if Robert mentions it again, which I'm sure he will."

"If he's a good friend, he will son. You stay safe, you hear." "Yes", echoed his Mom. "I will," he said, hugging them both. "I'll keep in touch by mail or phone. Try not to worry."

He knew they would worry until the whole scenario was over. Once Robert had shown Sam where his 'quarters' were, he broached the subject of paying him again. He wrote down a figure for each month and asked Sam what he thought. "Are you sure you want to pay me that much?"

"Of course, I'm sure. We agreed that figure as a family. We can afford it Sam. Please accept it. We're foregoing a holiday this year while all this is going on so this is part of what we'd have paid for that. We appreciate you taking on this job."

"Well I reckon I've got the best part of the deal. Thank you, I accept."

"Good," said Robert "That takes care of that. I'm glad you accept, after all, you're doing an important thing for us and we all feel safer now you're here."

"I'll set up my gear then I'll be good to go tonight. I usually drink coffee through the night as I don't sleep anyway. Could I ask you for some?"

"Sure. That's no problem. You'll find a coffee pot in the downstairs, by the sofa. I'll get Beth to make the pot up and it'll keep hot in the machine all night."

"Great, thank you. I'll sleep like a log in the morning with no bad dreams so it works out well. You'd think drinking all that coffee would keep me awake but it doesn't."

"Okay. Anything else you need?"

"Well, if it's not too much trouble a sandwich?"

"Of course, it's no trouble. Anything you don't like?"

"Just cheese, anything else is fine."

"Right, I'll get Beth to do those things for you tonight. I'll let you get settled in now."

Robert left the guest room and went back to the living room. The girls were both out now, being on afternoon shifts. They often said how incredible it was that they often had shifts that coincided. It was good though as it gave them a chance to see their respective boy-friends if they were off. Having a romantic life when you were on shifts was not easy but they managed it.

Robert told Beth the agreement and the couple of things Sam had asked for.

"He's a nice guy, I like him. I think this is going to work out well."

"Agreed", said Beth.

"We can't cover you during the day though, that worries me. We have to trust, Beth. The guys at work will keep an eye on me. They know the situation."

"Good," said Beth, "that's good to know. What is it you do for the Government exactly? You never did tell me."

"Beth, I can't tell you. It's classified is all I can tell you. Please trust me."

"I do. Quite important work then?"

"Yes, it is."

"I won't ask again Robert. No wonder you get paid so well."

Robert squeezed her. "Yes, it has its benefits."

The phone rang. Robert picked it up. "I'm sorry to call you when it's a weekend but I have some good news for you. The Assassin (the first one) that was after you is dead. I thought that would ease your mind." It was Captain Bedford.

"Thank you so much for letting me know," said Robert that's very welcome news. "Can you hold on please while I tell Beth?"

"Yeah, sure." He relayed the news to Beth. "We're both delighted," said Robert.

"About that other issue we talked about. There is definitely information leaking out. Have you had a chance to look at it yet?"

"Yes, I've started. My boss gave me the go ahead after you spoke with him. I've done four so far and they're clean."

"Right. I won't ask any more or your wife will get suspicious. I'll leave it to you to let me know."

"Will do, 'bye." Little did they know another Assassin would be sent after Robert as the first had failed....

10

The day came when Matt and Tim had to go to court. They had been kept in a safe-house prior to that. They were taken in a police car and ushered into court with nothing over their heads. The Police knew the Press would be ready and waiting. They did not have to face a Jury. This case was being dealt with by a Judge only. There was a Prosecutor and the boys had a Lawyer. Only their parents and Robert and Beth were present.

An Usher said "All stand for the Judge." They did so and then were told to sit down. The Judge asked the Prosecutor to put his case first.

"Your Honour, these boys were caught red-handed after they had committed a drive-by shooting. They have a history with Alfred Jones' gang, having joined them at ages ten and nine. They chose to do whatever the gang ordered them to do and, in this case, we can only be grateful that no-one was killed as my clients could have been standing by the window. We ask that they are dealt with by the full measure of the Law. They should not be on the streets anymore They are a danger to the public and totally untrustworthy. That concludes the State's Prosecution case."

"I'll hear the Defence now", said the Judge.

"Your Honour these boys were brought in by the gang for a reason. They wanted to groom kids young, the way terrorists do. They didn't realise what they were getting into. The parents have said that they have failed them by not always being there for them so the boys looked on the gang as a family. We admit that does not excuse what they have done and we know they will have to be punished but our concern is that if they are sent to the closed prison Alfred could get them killed. There is a very real risk of that. One solution would be to put them in the witness protection programme. We ask that the Court has mercy on these boys who were recruited deliberately. That concludes the Defence case." The Lawyer sat down.

The Judge addressed the boys. "Were you taught right from wrong?"

"Yes", your Honour," said Matt and Tim together.

"Then why did you do it?" questioned the Judge.

"It was like a second family and we got a high out of everything we did. I'm glad we've been caught. They would have started training us how to kill people next. We know what we did was wrong and we should be punished but please don't put us where Al or his gang can get to us or we're dead" said Matt.

The Judge picked up her pen and began to fiddle with it as she was thinking. "I don't believe in this case that the witness protection programme is appropriate", she said. "You two knew what you were doing and chose to do it. That's free-will. You had a choice. I appreciate that you were groomed young by the gang but if you hadn't been caught, I think you would have got a "high" out of killing and that concerns me greatly. You could have killed these people in court. No, I will not permit you to join the witness protection programme. You have to pay for what you've done."

Their Lawyer raised his hand. "Put your hand down Mr Darby, I'm not done yet." The Lawyer complied. "My decision is that you are taken to Belview Prison which is a Prison in the next State, where you will have the chance through hard work to learn a trade and be rehabilitated. Due to the gravity of both your cases you must be punished harshly. I sentence you to fourteen years there and hope when you come out you will be better members of Society. Court adjourned."

She administered her gravel and the matter was concluded. The boys were taken away by the police. Their mother was crying and their father looked white. Beth and Robert felt sorry for them but felt that justice had been done today. They made their way out of the court.

The Press were everywhere. "Can I get a comment from you?" asked an eager young journalist.

"Justice has been done," said Robert." They made their way through the huge crowd and went back to their car. "Well," said Robert, "I really hope that they will be safe there as it's in the next State from here and that they'll be rehabilitated. Their parents seem a reasonable couple. I feel sorry for them. Those kids were groomed. Still, they had a choice but maybe it was groomed out of them who knows? At least that's over."

"Yes", said Beth, "I feel sorry for the parents too. It's going to be a long journey for them to go visit as it's in the next State but I guess they could always stay some place overnight."

"Yes," said Robert. "We're still at risk, Beth. The gang will send more."

"I know but we have one small victory today that helps." They had reached the place where they had left their car. They got in and drove home in silence.

Craig and Joanna both had the day off which did not happen often. They had decided to have a picnic as it was a lovely day. Craig said he'd bring the coleslaw, as he made his own and Joanna adored it. They had decided to picnic on the beach. The beach at Sebastian's Peak was expansive. When the tide was out it was a good couple of miles wide and a similar length long-ways. It was beautiful the sand was white and the sea a turquoise and deep blue colour. If you climbed up to the top of the Peak you could look down and see right down to the bottom of the sea it was so clear. It really was a lovely place to live. They took a picnic with them and found a spot in the sand-dunes that were at the top of the beach. Craig put down the blanket while Joanna sorted out the picnic.

"This is lovely," said Joanna. "I finally get time to have you all to myself."

"Yes," agreed Craig, "with our schedules it's a nightmare to find time so let's make the most of it."

Joanna began to get the picnic out and lay it on the blanket. There were ham sandwiches, hard-boiled eggs, some apple pie with cream and Craig's homemade coleslaw. A flask of coffee and two bottles of soda were also included. They began to eat.

"Boy, I didn't realise how hungry I was," said Craig as he munched on a ham sandwich with the coleslaw.

"Me neither," said Joanna, "this is good coleslaw Craig."

"Family recipe," said Craig as he munched. They had soon

polished off all of the contents and were having a coffee which was steaming hot from the flask. "Jo," said Craig how are you all holding up with this gang thing?"

"We have a guy Dad knows staying in the guest room. He watches out overnight."

"That's good to know. If only the Police could stop all these gangs, we wouldn't see the things we do at work. Nothing prepares you for that. It doesn't get better with time, I guess that's what keeps us human."

"Yes," agreed Joanna. "I find it real hard telling the families that their loved one isn't gonna make it." She stared out at sea as though seeing the faces of their loved ones then snapped back to reality. She was with Craig and this was a day to enjoy.

"Jo," began Craig. "I need to ask you something."

"Yes?"

"We've been engaged now for two years. Will you marry me Jo - and soon?"

"Yes, Craig, I will." He had so expected her to say no and quote their work schedules that for a moment it didn't sink in. He looked stunned. Joanna looked at him and laughed. She tickled his face playfully. "Craig, I said yes."

He looked at her and cupped her face in his hands before he kissed her. "Does your family approve of me?"

"Yes, they think you're a lovely guy and they couldn't wish for a better son-in-law. My Mom asked me the other day when you were going to pop the question." They both laughed. It felt so good to be discussing their future and not their work continually. "What about your parents?"

"They feel the same as yours. I'm so glad. At last we can focus on us. Do you want a large wedding?"

"No. Just immediate family and good friends. How about you?"

"That suits me fine. After all it's about us and big weddings have a habit of getting out of hand. One of my mates had a big wedding and he noticed someone there he'd never seen before. He asked who she was and it turned out she wasn't anybody's relative she just liked going to weddings. Apparently, she'd scan the papers to see when weddings were on and attend them. Nobody ever noticed before. So, I don't want our wedding advertised. Agreed?"

"Agreed."

"I'm gonna have to ask your Dad's permission of course. When do you think would be a good time to ask him?"

"Anytime to be honest. What we've got 'going on' isn't going away in a hurry so whenever you like."

"You think tonight would be too soon?"

"No. I'm sure both my parents would welcome some good news."

"Well, all right then I'll ask him tonight! I'm so happy, I thought you'd mention our schedules again."

"I figure if we've managed to keep our love life going for two years, we can do it for real in a marriage. I'm really happy Craig, I love you so much."

"Same here. Come here." He held her tight and they hugged and kissed for what seemed like forever. Then he let her go. "Let's go for a walk on the beach and talk more about our future, a house or apartment - all of that stuff. I can't wait to ask your Dad."

They packed away all the picnic items and rolled up the blanket and left them in the dunes where they could see them. They had four hours before Robert and Beth would be home so the afternoon was theirs to enjoy until the sea returned. The sun shone brightly and its radiance surrounded them as if giving its approval.

Evening came and they loaded up the picnic and blanket into Craig's convertible, leaving the roof down for it was still hot. He rang his parents before driving to tell them the good news and put it on speaker phone so Joanna could hear how excited they were. Then Craig drove straight to Joanna's home. Both Beth's and Robert's car were there. Joanna let herself in with Craig in tow. Beth was the first one to notice Craig. Joanna winked at her Mom who got the message and nodded back.

"Come in Craig it's lovely to see you. Did you both have a good afternoon?"

"We sure did Mom."

"Sit down and make yourself at home Craig. Do either of you want anything to eat?" They both said they were still full from the picnic. Beth called to Robert. He came into the living room and welcomed Craig. After all the pleasantries were over, Craig gathered up his courage.

"I want to ask you something Robert. Joanna and I want to get married. Will you give us your blessing?"

"Well it's about time," said Robert. "Of course, you have my blessing. We couldn't wish for a better man for our daughter."

"We don't want a big wedding Mom," interrupted Joanna so filled with excitement.

"We can work on all the details later. Welcome to the family Craig."

11

The Assassin had tried getting out of bed. They were in their room having spent two weeks in ICU. Their legs were wobbly and didn't feel like their own. They stumbled and fell. Fortunately for them a nurse was passing by and saw them on the floor.

"What are you doing out of bed?" she asked crossly "I have to get another nurse and we have to hoist you back into bed. Are you hurt? I'm sorry, I should have asked you that first." She pressed the assist button on the call bell to get another nurse.

"No, I'm not hurt", said the Assassin. "Just feeling really weak. I'm sorry I thought I'd be able to get out of bed easily, obviously not. I'm not hurt just embarrassed."

The nurse to assist came quickly. "I'll get the hoist," she said. A few minutes later she brought in something that looked like a horse with no head. "Now we have to put some straps under your legs and over your head and arms then we can safely get you into bed."

The Assassin was duly strapped up and then lifted into the air and steered into position over their bed. The nurses undid the straps and between them they got the Assassin back into bed.

"Now please don't do that again," said the first nurse sounding kinder this time, as she pulled up the summer quilt.

"You stay put and we'll get the Doctor to come in and see you." The Doctor arrived a short time afterwards.

"I hear you've been trying to stretch your legs," he said. "I'm afraid you'll be with us for two more weeks to recover. You don't know how ill you've been. We nearly lost you one night. You'll just have to enjoy our hospitality as best you can."

The Assassin began to protest. "What about my job?"

"Yes, we thought about that and I rang your agency. They said you'll still have the job in two weeks so not to worry. Now you've pulled out some monitors I had on you so I'll get a nurse to come in and redo the wiring." I've had stubborn patients like you before so don't do that again. I know, you're impatient but it will do you no good at all. You'll just set yourself back. You could have broken a leg. I'm sure the nurses told you off. Please take this as a stern warning. You'll get better quicker that way. Okay?"

"I'm sorry," said the Assassin. "I thought I could do it. I couldn't believe it when I fell." "Well I hope you'll stay in bed now and you'll get your strength back in a couple of weeks," he said kindly. "Stop worrying about your job I've seen executives here before always worrying about their jobs." If only he knew thought the Assassin. "I'll get a nurse now to come and re-wire you. I know they were more concerned about getting you in bed than doing that. Behave yourself!" He tried to look stern then just laughed and the Assassin joined him.

"I will", said the Assassin. They had never felt so weak. The only other times were when they had the normal childhood illnesses. The Doctor left and a nurse came in to do the instructed job.

"I hear you had an accident," she said.

Oh boy another telling off is coming, thought the Assassin but it didn't.

"How are you feeling?" she asked.

"Like I've been hit by a truck," said the Assassin.

"Yes, you've been very poorly. Rest and you'll be fine."

"Everyone keeps telling me that," said the Assassin.

"Well maybe it'll sink in," she said laughing. "You'll be fine you'll see. There, you're all wired up again. Would you like something to drink and maybe a snack?"

The Assassin did feel hungry now that she'd mentioned it. "Yes, that would be great, thank you." Before long she returned with a tray laden with a selection of snacks and a coffee.

"Do you take cream and sugar with your coffee? she asked.

"Yes please," said the Assassin. Everyone was being so kind the Assassin hadn't experienced much kindness since they'd been doing their job. They felt a lump coming up in their throat.

"Thank you, this is great."

"Right then. I'll leave you to enjoy them. Try to get some sleep if you can after you've had those." She left the room and the Assassin tucked in to the snacks and drank the coffee. Then they realised they were rather tired and slipped into a pleasant sleep, soon sleeping deeply, too deep for the nightmares to return.

12

Captain Bedford had arranged for Robert to meet him in his office. In due time Robert arrived with all the files in his brief-case.

"Let's have a coffee before we get down to business," said Captain Bedford.

"That would be good," said Robert.

They both drank in silence then the Captain broached the subject.

"Well Robert, you've been through all the files. Who is it?"

"I can't give you a clear answer Sir. Here's your file by the way. I hope your computer is okay."

"I would never have known anyone had hacked it if you hadn't told me. You're good at your job Robert, now what's the verdict?"

"No-one has got an off-shore account. There's not any more money coming in to any of your officer's accounts. All of them are getting paid what they should. The only thing that caught my eye was Officer Collins' spending. He seems to be able to afford more than he has coming in. His credit cards are not maxed out. But the amounts he's spending on the cards don't match with what he's getting paid. My conclusion is that he may be hiding money somewhere and not banking it or he's had a cash legacy which he hasn't banked yet, though that sounds improbable."

"Collins eh, yes there has been something though I thought nothing of it at the time. He came in with a very expensive watch on. I thought maybe it had been bought for him. So, we'll keep an eye on him. I'll need you to keep his file and a check every two weeks should do it. I don't want him getting suspicious but I need to know what his spending is. I know he owns a speed boat. He may be hiding money in there somewhere. When we have enough evidence, I'll consider what to do. We don't want to let him become suspicious or we'll tip our hand too early."

"Agreed," said Robert. "I'll do what you ask and keep you informed."

"Thank you," said the Captain. "By the way, as we're working together dispense with the formalities and call me John."

"Thank you, Sir, I mean John," said Robert.

"I knew we had a leak," said John "I was hoping I was wrong. Collins is a very likeable person. It's a shame if it turns out to be him. He had a promising career ahead of him."

"I hope I'm wrong," said Robert "but I can't see how he can afford what he has unless the money is somewhere else."

"I'll try feeding him some false information. I'll get all the Officers together and tell them all the same thing then we'll see what happens. Mitch is in place by the way. When we arrested the twelve men it made it easier for Mitch to get in. He'll let us know if the leak proves true. One of the men did crack and gave us some useful information in exchange for a deal. The lawyers will sort that out. Apparently, the gang have five houses here in Sebastian's Peak. He gave us a sketch and showed us on it where they are. They are all three-story buildings and pretty large. They usually have twelve or more living in them to do all the "work" Roger wants done. Roger moves around so it's hard to catch him. I plan to do another raid at a later date when Mitch gets us the information out about where Roger is. How is your man settling in by the way and has he noticed anything at night?"

"Not yet but we feel safer having him. The family all took to him at once. He's a very likeable guy and adores Beth's cooking." They both laughed.

"Well Robert thanks for the information. I mustn't keep you too late. You'll be wanting to get home."

"You're welcome Sir, I mean John. I'll keep in touch. We don't know if any more attacks are coming our way either, we're hoping not, so I hope to not be contacting you about that."

"I hope not too. Now get on home to that wife of yours.

"Thank you, John, I will." Robert got up and they both shook hands then Robert left his office and made his way home.

Captain Bedford got up to leave the office. He was a widower, his wife having died two years ago. The house felt empty without her but he had a number of good friends all of whom would invite him over for meals and to share their company. He also loved to go fishing and had a friend who would go with him. The friend had a boat and they would speed out to sea and see who could get the biggest catch. He felt blessed that way and knew that there was always a friend he could ring if he needed to. The news that he had a potential dirty cop saddened him greatly. He had come to trust all his officers over the years but his suspicions had proved to be true. He liked Collins. That made it worse. Collins had only been with them for a year but he'd made a good addition to the team and did his job well. The Captain wondered now if he had been 'planted' to infiltrate the police as Mitch was doing in Al's gang. The pieces fitted together neatly. He picked up his coat and left the office. There was a retired Captain whom he had served under he could call and he knew he would keep it confidential. He may just give him a call.

Josephine was not herself. She knew something was wrong in her relationship with Alex but couldn't put her finger on it. When she got home, she sought out her Mom. "Mom, can I talk to you?"

"You know you always can. Just let's have supper then we'll talk."

"Okay." She ate supper half-heartedly and Beth could tell her daughter was troubled. When the dish-washer was loaded and all was done with supper, she asked what was wrong.

"It's Alex Mom."

"Okay, what's wrong?"

"It's not easy to put my finger on it. He seems very interested in what we are going through and wants all the details. I know it may just be concern but he seems more interested in that than in me. I tried breaking the relationship off but he won't. He begged me for another chance. I really don't want to do that but it's hard. I don't trust him, but I've grown to love him. I'm beginning to think that he was 'told' by some-one to get close to me."

Alarm bells went off in Beth's head. Al's gang could have sent someone to get information on them.

"Mom," said Josephine, "do you think he's a 'plant?'" She thought her Mom may say she'd been reading too many detective books but she was silent for a moment.

"It is possible," said Beth. "How long is it you've been together now?"

"Seven months."

"It makes sense," said Beth. "I was hoping you'd think of that too."

"We'll tell your Dad and Sam. They'll have a good idea if that could be true. I'll get them both." Josephine waited while her Mom went to get them. The thought that Alex could be involved with the Gang was sickening. Why had she grown to love him? Her Dad and Sam arrived and sat down opposite her. She repeated her story to them. Robert's blood was up to think that anyone was hurting his daughter.

Sam looked at it logically and said, "He's sounding like trouble to me but if he won't let you break it off the best thing to do is tell the police about it. In fact, I think you should anyway with all that's going on. How do you feel about that?"

"I'll do it."

"Yes, I agree Jo," said Robert. "When are you supposed to see Alex again?"

"At the weekend."

"That gives us three days. I'll tell Captain Bedford you want to speak with him before then and we'll see if he agrees."

"I don't know why Alex would do it, said Josephine, "he gets a good wage unless someone's offered him more."

"It's possible," said Robert "money talks to people's egos."

"I'm sorry to offer bad news when you have a wedding to help plan," said Josephine, "but he's been bugging me. We're not like Jo and Craig. I can't see any future in it."

I only wish there was, she thought. "You were right to tell us" said Beth.

Robert agreed. "I'll ring the Captain in the morning," said Robert. "The sooner he knows the better." He couldn't tell them about his earlier conversation with Captain Bedford but pieces were beginning to come together in Robert's mind the way they had in Captain Bedford's mind when he learned about the dirty cop. He wondered if Alex had a computer that he could maybe try to hack but that was probably going a bit too far at the moment. "How are you Jo?"

"I'm confused and quite angry if I'm being used," said Josephine. "I'll do what you say and talk to the Captain in the morning. I'm on a late shift so I can."

Beth hugged her then got up and served the coffee. They would wait and see what tomorrow would bring.

The next day Josephine went with Robert to see Captain Bedford. Josephine repeated the story she had told her parents. Captain Bedford looked at Robert and Robert looked at him as if reading each other's minds. "I'm sorry to say that it sounds very probable that he's a plant. Can you bear to keep him close for a little longer? I have an idea that I want to try out, then we'll know for sure."

"I guess so," said Joanna. "but I really am beginning to despise him because I love him."

"I get what you're saying," said the Captain, "but if you could manage another month it would help, that's all I ask. Do you think you could bear that?"

"If it would help, I guess I could but I may have to act it out somehow" said Josephine."

"That's all I ask Josephine," said the Captain. "Thank you for telling me this. I have a plan that may just flush him out if he is a plant." They got up to leave. "Robert, did you both come together or in separate cars?"

"In separate cars, Jo has to get home and sleep, if she can, she's on a late shift. "Josephine, I hope you won't think me rude, but I could do with speaking with your Dad for a while. Are you okay with that?"

"Sure," said Josephine. She left the room and Captain Bedford asked Robert if he wanted some coffee while they talked. Robert assented.

"Well, are you thinking along the same lines that I am?" asked the Captain.

"Yes, I am," said Robert. "If you don't mind me asking, how are you going to flush him out?"

"I plan to get my officers together later today and tell them we know where Roger is and we'll make a plan of action later this week. Mitch will let us know by the end of the week if that information has been acted on. If Roger's moved again, Mitch will tell us. That will flush out Collins and Alex if they are associated with the gang. According to the information I get from Mitch that will determine what action I take. I may just raid a house or two just to keep them from becoming suspicious. I want Roger, he's the Deputy. All the orders come from him. He's eluded us so far but we will get him."

"I hope you do," said Robert. "I was thinking of hacking Alex's computer but I'd need an e-mail from Jo to get the address. She may get suspicious. I don't know what to do. I could maybe get it when she's out but I feel awful doing that."

"You may as well wait and see what happens this week then act Robert."

"You're right John. I just feel antsy as it's my daughter. I feel I should be doing something."

"I understand that," said John. "I'd feel the same. Do what you think is right for you. We would get a better idea if you did."

"Yeah, I have to wrestle with my conscience over that."

"I'll keep you in the loop Robert."

"Thank you, John, I appreciate that." Robert got up and shook the Captain's hand then left his office.

Three nights later, Sam was looking through his night vision camera when he noticed a van pull up behind Robert's car. It had its rear doors so that they backed on to Roberts boot. Sam began taking photos. Three men got out and one of them began to pick the lock on Robert's car boot. He got the boot open. Then two of the others dragged a body out of the van and put it in Robert's boot then pulled it back down. Their job done, the men got back into the van and drove off. Sam had got a picture of the whole sequence. It was obvious they were trying to frame Robert for a murder and if Sam had not been in place the frame would have worked. Doubtless the next day the police would get an anonymous call giving the details. Sam re-played the sequence on his camera. He had the licence plate of the van, though it may have been stolen. The three men he had no faces of unfortunately, just white outlines of features. He would go to the local chemist who also did photos tomorrow and get them blown up to ten inches by eight to give more detail and let the Police have them. Soon, the family were up and Sam took Robert aside and showed him his photos.

"It may be best if I speak to Captain Bedford first" said Robert. He dialled the number and explained the situation.

"We'll play along when we get the call," said Captain Bedford. "They'll have someone watching your house, we'll let them see you taken away in handcuffs then we'll get you back after dark. I'll speak to your Boss and see if we can get you working at home for a few weeks. Do you have a study where you can work?"

"Yes, I do."

"That's fine then. Don't worry, we'll find the men who did this. There will be finger prints on your car boot and on the body unless they wore gloves of course. I'll get Forensics on it once we get the anonymous call. Could Sam make out any faces?"

"Not on his camera but he'll be getting ten inches by eight so there may be more to see."

"Okay Robert, sit tight and we'll get you in due time today. We'll make it look real, and if anyone phones in pretending to be a lawyer or wanting any information, I have a woman Police Officer I can trust to answer the phone. In case you're wondering how that will work it's simple. Anything to do with you will be put through to my officer. We'll make them think their plan worked then publish the photos so you can be 'let out'. That should shake them up a bit. Get some rest now and try not to worry."

"Thanks, I'll do my best." The call ended and Robert went to tell his family the news. "They really are despicable," said Beth. "If we hadn't had Sam here you couldn't have proved your innocence. Thank God you got him."

"Amen to that."

Sam got back with the photos. Josephine had driven him, as his car was in the garage. Later that morning, they heard the blare of police sirens arriving. The officers came in. Robert showed them the photos. They said they'd get them to Captain Bedford and that they would be taking Robert to the police station for 'show.' They took him out in hand-cuffs and loaded him into a police car. They sped away to the police station. The Forensics team asked for Robert's car key so that they could examine everything carefully. Beth handed him the keys and when they left, although she knew it was not real, she burst into tears. The girls were working, so couldn't offer their support but Sam was there to comfort her.

"Don't you worry Ma'am," he said, "he'll be home tonight. We have the photos of what happened. I had two copies of all the photos made up in case theirs get lost. We can prove his innocence."

"I know, I'm sorry it's not been easy these past few months but I am so grateful you were here, otherwise there would have been no way to prove it."

Meanwhile, a car had been hiding out of sight further up the road. The long lens guy was back and the lens came out when Robert was arrested. He reeled them off then, satisfied that he had enough, put the camera down and began to drive off. He had what he needed. The gang would be very pleased to see that their plan was working. Very pleased indeed.

Later that evening, a police car drew up outside the Johnson's home with two policemen in uniform in it. Beth let them in and was delighted to see that one of them was Robert.

"We have a man coming around to your back entrance who will change clothes with Robert," said the officer. "Ah, I hear a tapping on your back door. That will be him now."

Beth let the other officer in. "This was the Captain's idea in case anyone was still watching."

"Thank you so much," said Beth, "I wondered how you were going to get him back." "We'll just change clothes," said the Officer "then we'll have to hang around for a while to make it look as though we're doing something. Would you happen to have some coffee handy?"

"Of course," said Beth. The men went into Robert's study to change while Beth got the coffee pot on. While the men were changing one of the officers told Robert that the Captain would be releasing the photos Sam took to the Press in two weeks as he wanted to know the gang's response. Robert's boss had been told and a man would be bringing in Robert's computer in the morning, again using the back entrance. Once changed, they all enjoyed a cup of coffee.

"I've got the Captain's e-mail address here. He asked if Sam could send him the video of what happened along with the stills," said one of the Officers.

"Sure," said Robert, "I'm so glad I had that evidence or their frame would have worked."

"Yeah," said one of the officers, "it would have too." They enjoyed their coffee and had a chat then, when they had been there for thirty minutes, they left.

"Well Beth it's good to be home. Are the girls home?"

"Joanna is but she's out with Craig. Josephine's on a late so she's sleeping at the moment."

"Okay," said Robert, come here." Beth sat on the sofa beside him and he held her close.

13

The Assassin was now fully recovered. They left the hospital and rented a room in a hotel so that they could review their progress. Another long plane flight was ahead of them. That meant a few days in a hotel to recover from jet-lag. They had been given a list of hotels so they could call ahead and secure a room. They would then have another plane to catch which would land at an airport a long distance from Sebastian's Peak, so they would have to rent a car for the final journey and that would take a long time. It had taken days to get to where they were now. Sometimes they would have to stay in a hotel longer if they didn't feel fully recovered. The Agency had made allowances for that and as long as their agents kept them updated there were no problems. This contract had taken so long to fill, they almost felt like giving up but that was not in their code. They would continue to hunt their prey until the job was done.

14

The Johnson's neighbours had stayed away but one of them came over the next day to see if Beth needed anything. Robert quickly hid.

"It's very kind of you," said Beth "but we are coping okay. We know Robert's innocent and soon the truth will come out."

"The other neighbours wanted me to see you on their behalf. None of us believe it. Please let Robert know that when you see him."

"I will" said Beth. "Can I offer you a coffee?"

"No, thank you. Well I guess that's all I came to tell you," said the neighbour.

"Thank you and please thank the other neighbours for me."

"Will do." He left and Robert came out of hiding.

"Did you hear all that?" asked Beth.

"I did. It's good to know they all know me well enough to trust me."

Robert knew that Beth would need to leave for school soon, the neighbour had been early. It was only seven thirty, but they knew she got up early. She picked up her packed lunch, kissed Robert goodbye then left to get in her car. Once she had gone, Robert made his way into Josephine's room feeling very guilty. He opened her laptop, fired it up, then scrolled through her files until he found an e-mail from Alex. He jotted down the address, then closed everything down after leaving it the way he had found it. He took the address to the study then sat at his desk and got his work computer out. It would have to be locked in its case when not in use for security reasons. He entered Alex's e-mail address then started to hack it, looking for any money that had come in or any that had been put in an off-shore account. He found that Alex had indeed come into money but had left it in an investment account in his bank. That puzzled Robert, as it was hidden in plain sight. If anyone was to investigate further, they would soon find it. He thought maybe it had been a legacy as it wasn't a huge sum. He would let Captain Bedford know and see what he thought. They were only looking at three thousand dollars, but Alex may not have been working for them for long. A puzzled Robert continued to hack. Then he saw a fire-wall he recognised. He continued to hack and soon found out what he wanted to know. He put the address in the desk's top drawer and locked it. Then he started on the work his Boss had sent him via his computer.

⊕

Meanwhile, in prison Al was having a wonderful time. All the inmates were terrified of him and whatever Al wanted Al got. A prisoner was being admitted to prison who happened to be taller and stronger than Al. He had already decided that he would be top dog and once he was processed, he went to look at the competition. He had more muscle power than Al from years of working out. He would take him down when they were next allowed out. He was put in a cell with room-mate Donald Muller. Once it was time for them all to go outside he determined to take Al down.

"I don't believe we've met," he said. "I'm Bo and that stands for Boss. One of us is going down today and it won't be me."

The men made a circle so the two men could fight. Al made a run at Bo that should have taken him down. It didn't. He tried again. This time, one of the men had given him a prison-made knife called a shiv. Al made a run and pointed the shiv where it was supposed to be fatal. Bo knocked it out of his hand. Al knew he was in trouble. He had never met anyone as strong as this man. He tried beating his fists on Bo but Bo just pushed him off. For Bo, this was a cat and mouse game where Al was his prey, it was only a matter of time. He would let Al wear himself out then he'd take him. The prisoners were terrified. The guards on the towers paid little attention since the fight had only been initiated by one man. Soon Al was worn out.

"Okay Bo you're the new Boss."

"Yes, I am," said Bo "but we're not finished yet. I believe it's my turn." He strode over to Al pulled him up in the air then threw him down.

"I get the point" said Al "you're the new Boss I've told you already."

"Ah but I have to take you down I'm afraid."

Calmly and efficiently he picked Al up and broke his neck. He left him on the floor for the guards to see. They soon picked up on it and prison officers were sent to hand-cuff Bronco and take him to the Prison Governor. To be honest, thought the Governor, he had never had a prisoner as large as Bronco Hayden.

"Twenty days in isolation plus hard labour when you get out," he said. "You've not made a very good start here. I hope you'll behave better when your time in isolation is up."

"You can count on it," said Bronco.

"Good, good. Okay officer, take him away."

Bronco was used to isolation. He would use the time to keep himself fit. He had been involved in crime since he was young, having been thrown from one foster home to another. His parents were dead, having been killed in a house fire with Bronco being the only survivor. He had never had the benefit of being in any good foster homes so he was not properly taught right from wrong. He found a local gang near one of the homes and joined that, so he behaved better so he could stay in the neighbourhood. He was twelve when he first learned the thrill of crime as long as you didn't get caught. Then, as the years passed, he graduated into serious crime and had to hide his stolen money well away from the foster parents' eyes. He had pried one of the floorboards loose and hid it under there. When he was old enough, he was taken out of the system so he spent all his time with the gang he had grown up with and the serious crime began.

FOURTEEN DAYS LATER

The papers were full of the photographs of Robert that Sam had taken. The Police came out with Robert and moved him through the crowds of Press into a Police car. All this had been pre-arranged as Robert was supposedly in Police custody. They drove him home and one of the officers said how relieved Robert must be.

"I certainly am," said Robert, "but all of you knew I was secretly at home. I have to say I wouldn't like to spend fourteen days in one of your cells."

"Well, you're home now," said the Officer. There were Press outside the house.

"No comment," said Robert as he moved through the crowd. Beth was waiting at the front door and ushered him in speedily.

"Well, that worked well," said Robert gratefully. He knew the Captain would want to see him later that day. Robert had gone through all the officers' files now and a picture had begun to emerge. Beth made him a cup of coffee and brought in some freshly baked chocolate chip cookies. "You've been busy darling," said Robert.

"I made them early this morning," said Beth. "It's a homecoming gift, enjoy sweetheart."

Robert kissed her, held her close then released her and they both sat on the sofa and enjoyed the cookies and coffee.

"You know I have to see Captain Bedford shortly. I'm sorry darling but I have to see him in my office. It's classified."

"No problem," said Beth, "I'm not going in to school today. They gave me the day off."

"Well, that's good off them after all, everyone believed the lie."

"Yes, and it would have worked if it hadn't been for Sam," said Robert.

"He's sleeping like a log at the moment. He came to tell me, as I'm home too. Thank goodness we have him."

"Yeah, I do," said Robert. There was a ring on the doorbell and Beth went to answer it. It was Captain Bedford.

"I won't take up too much of Robert's time," he said.

"Do you want a coffee and some cookies?" asked Beth.

"That would be lovely," said the Captain. He sat down with them and they chatted and enjoyed the coffee and cookies. Then, when they had all had enough, Robert got up and told Beth that he and the Captain had better get down to business. Robert led the way to his office.

"Do sit down Sir, I mean John. It takes a bit of getting used to."

The Captain laughed, then said, "What have you found out?"

"Well, Alex was a bit of a mystery until I hit a firewall that I've recognised before. I managed to hack through it and it turns out he's a Fed."

"What?!"

"Yes, he's obviously been assigned to Josephine as she doesn't have a boyfriend."

"I wonder why Jake didn't keep me in the loop. May I borrow your phone?"

"Sure."

The Captain dialled a number. "Hello, is Jake there please? It's Captain Bedford." A few minutes passed then Jake picked up the phone.

"Hello John, what can I do for you?"

"I've been suspicious of a young man named Alex Garner. He's been hanging around Josephine Johnson for a number of months now and seems to be milking her for information re her family. She wants out of the relationship but he wants another chance. I wonder if you could look into it for me?"

Jake sighed then said, "You should have been told. I've been doing under-cover work or I would have told you. He's a Fed. We assigned him to Josephine as she had no boyfriend. He's there to keep her safe. I'm real sorry you weren't told."

"That explains it, thank you Jake. At least now I know, I feel re-assured. May I tell the family?"

"Sure. We want Josephine to be at ease with him."

"Right. I'll let them know, "thanks Jake." He put down the receiver. "Well, I can let you all know what the position is so I suggest we go back down and let your wife know. Is Josephine in?"

"No, she's on an early. She'll come back here to sleep. I'll let her know when she comes in. It will relieve her mind."

They descended the stairs to where Beth was preparing lunch.

"Would you both like some coffee now?" They both said they would and once the coffee was served, Robert told Beth what had been discovered about Alex. "I can't say how grateful I am to hear that," said Beth.

"Jo will have peace of mind now knowing he's there to protect her. It's a huge relief," said Robert." When they had finished their coffee, the Captain got up to go.

"Do stay for a meal Captain if you have the time?" Beth said. The Captain was overcome by the kindness of this family. "That would be an honour," he said.

When he had left the family, the Captain went back to his office and got out a yellow legal pad. He began to draw a plan on it so that they could do another raid on the houses where they knew the gang were. He had told all the officers a couple of days ago that they knew where Roger was and waited to see what he got back from Mitch which would tell him if they had a leak. He'd left a message on the Captain's voice-mail. Roger had moved again but this time, they did know where. He would have to be careful that Collins didn't catch on that they had an under-cover cop in the gang. So, he planned the raid to cover every one of the houses they knew of. Today, he would phone everyone else he wanted included in the plan including the Feds, and he wanted helicopters and snipers. This was to be a huge attack. He would box them in so there was no means of escape this time. He wanted Roger, period. His phone rang. He picked up the receiver.

"Yeah?"

"This is the Governor from Death Row. We have to inform you that Alfred Jones met his death at the hands of another prisoner. He won't be in charge of the gang anymore."

"Thanks for letting me know," said the Captain. He shouted "YES!" and didn't care who heard him. This was the snake's head cut off. Roger was good but he took his orders from Al. How he got the information out of prison was still a mystery that they hadn't resolved. Now would be a testing time for Roger but the Captain hoped they'd get him before he'd had a chance to flex his muscles.

Josephine came home after her shift knowing she had a date with Alex. "I'm not sure I want to go, Mom," she said.

"I think you should," said Beth, "I think you should listen to what he has to say."

"Do you know something then, that I don't?"

"We do, and it's good news. You'll feel better when you come home, promise." "Okay, I'll go but I can't imagine what he's been hiding."

"You'll see, now go get ready." Beth shushed her out of the room to the stairs. "Something's got into you Mom but I can't think what it is, I'm going to my room. Away with you Mother," said Josephine laughingly. It didn't take long for Josephine to get ready. She was curious about what Alex had to say as she drove to her destination. She entered the restaurant where Alex was already waiting. He got up and moved her chair for her. When she was seated Alex ordered some drinks then took her hand into his.

"I have something I need to tell you. I'm a Fed. I've been assigned to you because you had no boyfriend. I was to be there to keep you safe and find out how your family was coping but I've got feelings for you. I love you Jo."

Once she got over the shock Josephine sat in silence for moment.

"I didn't think you cared about me at all. That's why I tried to break it off. I never dreamed you had feelings for me and that you were a Fed."

"Yes, I do have feelings for you."

"That's all I wanted to hear," said Alex. "Now stand up."

"What?"

"Just do it." She did as he said and he moved closer to her, held her in his arms, and began to kiss her. It was a long, deep kiss. Josephine felt her back arching backwards. When he had finished, the whole restaurant full of diners began clapping. They both sat down. "Think I love you now?" said Alex.

"That was some kiss!" admitted Josephine. "Yes, I believe you and I do have strong feelings for you."

"Why don't you admit you love me too? That kiss wasn't a one-way effort and you know it."

"All right I have to admit I've never been kissed like that before, and yes, I believe I love you."

"That's all I wanted to hear" said Alex. "Now I guess we should order some food." He picked up the menu and began to scan it. "What do you like the look of?" Josephine had picked up her menu and it had photos in it of the various dishes. She was still recovering from that kiss.

"The steak will be fine please and not the huge one."

"Fair enough." He held up his hand for the waitress.

"Yes, Sir. Are you ready to order now?"

"We are. One T Bone Steak small, and one larger."

"Do you want that with all the trimming and how do you want it cooked?"

Alex looked at Josephine. She said, "Well done please and yes all the trimmings, thanks."

"And you Sir?"

"Yes, all the trimmings and well done please."

"Okay I'll get that ordered for you Sir. It shouldn't be long."

"Thanks," said Alex. He looked at Josephine, "Are you okay?"

"Yes, I'm still reeling from that kiss. I've had feelings for you for some time but when you kept milking me about my parents it put me off. Why didn't you tell me earlier you silly man?"

"I thought it would put you off me." He picked up her hand again and squeezed it. "Now you know can we date often?"

"Yes, we can and if you kiss me like that again tonight, I won't stop you." They both laughed. Shortly, their steaks arrived and they both tucked in.

"I didn't realise how hungry I was," said Alex.

"Me neither," said Josephine. They finished their meal and then Alex asked if she wanted a dessert. "Just mixed fruit salad please."

"Okay, and I'll have the chipped cookie ice cream."

"Ooh that sounds good. Make that a double." He did as she

requested and when they saw the size of them, they realised they could both have shared one! They did the best they could then finally gave up. They had been laughing and joking together and finally Josephine felt relaxed with him. She saw him now first as a man and second a Fed. That he loved her was clear and she knew he was a man she could rely on. She knew now that she deeply loved him too and told him so.

"I'm so grateful to hear that. I've had something in my pocket for the last two months. I hope you won't think me too forward. I haven't spoken to your father yet."

He got down on one knee and took a ring in a box from his pocket and said: "Jo, will you marry me?" The whole restaurant of diners was watching again. She knew that kiss had proved she loved him. Everyone was sitting very quietly for her answer. Oh, what the heck thought Jo why not live dangerously!

"Yes, I will." All the diners in the restaurant were applauding again. Alex looked as if he'd expected her to say no as it was a bit early. When he heard her say "Yes" he got up and punched the air.

"YES!" shouted Alex. "Yes!" shouted back the diners, still clapping. Josephine felt her face flushing but didn't care. At last something wonderful was happening to her. She heard Alex ordering champagne. The waiter arrived with the bottle on ice.

"Do you want it opened now or later?" asked the waiter.

"Now please," said Alex. When the cork flew from the bottle every one clapped again and someone said: "Good for you." Many echoed that. The diners were clearly enjoying the entertainment.

Alex got up and said: "Thank you to all of you." The waiter started to pour the champagne. "We'll only drink some of this," said Alex. "We have to drive home. So, can you re-cork what we don't drink?"

"Sure Sir."

"Thank you." They both held their glasses up and toasted each other then waited for the fizz to go down before drinking it. Josephine's mind was reeling. It had all been so sudden but that kiss was a two-way one and she knew her parents must know something about it all. That made it easier. The restaurant owner declared to the waiting audience that the meal was on the house. The diners clapped again. One of the diners had a hat on. He took it off put a few dollars in it and passed it round. When the other diners had added their contribution, they had a good amount there. The man with the hat asked for it back then he presented the dollars to Alex. "Something to go towards your wedding from us all. We wish you both great happiness." He put his hat on again and sat down.

"We don't know how to thank you," said Alex "but we are really grateful and appreciate this gift very much. Our thanks to all of you."

Both he and Josephine clapped them all. When they had finished the owner of the restaurant said, "Our thanks to you for such an entertaining evening." Once Alex and Josephine had finished their meal, they got up to leave. All the diners clapped them until they were out of the door.

"Oh Alex," said Josephine, "what a wonderful evening. Why didn't you tell me you were a Fed? I was worried you were a 'plant' from the other side." She poked him in the ribs playfully.

"I was under orders until you started sniffing around. Then they told me I could tell you and your family."

"Fair enough," said Josephine. They got to his car and got in. He reached out for her and embraced her in a kiss again. When they had finished, Alex said he had better get her home.

"Are you coming in?" she asked still reeling from the kiss. She knew now that this was the man she would marry and she was bursting with happiness.

"Not tonight Jo. I have to meet a fellow agent at midnight would you believe! I will ask your father's blessing tomorrow night if that's okay?"

"Oh, all right then," said Josephine feeling some disappointment but still reeling from the kiss.

"I've loved you for months," said Alex, "but I couldn't tell you. That was hard. At least it's out in the open now."

They arrived at Josephine's home and kissed again. "Yes, this is the man for me," thought Josephine. She got out of the car and walked on air until she got to the door and let herself in. Her Mom was sitting in the living room sewing and her Dad must obviously be in the study.

"Mom," her mother looked up."

"Yes Jo?"

She went and sat beside her Mom flashing the ring. Josephine recited all the evening's events.

"It was that kiss Mom, that's when I knew I loved him. What a kiss, it made me arch my back. The whole evening was like something you see at the movies."

"Well," said Beth "it looks as though we'll be planning a double wedding. I'm so pleased for you. We know he'll look after you. Oh, here's your Dad coming down the stairs. You can tell him while I put the coffee pot on. Josephine again explained all that had happened.

"That's wonderful," said Robert, "he's a good man. He's been protecting you all these months. We set aside some money for your weddings in a high interest account. It should have made good interest by now. Especially as there are two of you to be thinking of. It will be a double wedding I assume?"

"Oh yes. You know Jo and I have always done things together. When is she due in?" "Around one in the morning."

"I'll wait up for her. I'm too excited to sleep."

"Okay."

"Oh, I forgot to tell you. Alex will be calling in tomorrow evening to ask for your blessing."

"Well I think I can do that."

"Thanks Dad."

"I'm just glad your sister and you have found good men. Well, it's half past twelve so your Mother and I will be going up to bed. You won't have too long to wait for Joanna. Goodnight." He kissed the top of her head and made for the bedroom. Josephine waited until she heard the key in the lock. She had to restrain herself until her sister was properly in. Joanna knew that whatever Josephine wanted to tell her was important.

"Okay," she said, "what's happened?"

Josephine again related what had happened that evening. There were squeals of delight from the both of them.

"Oh, said Joanna "we'll have a double wedding! It's so exciting."

"Yes," said Josephine. "It was that kiss that did it. What a kiss."

"It sounds like you had a wonderful evening."

"Oh, we did. I decided to live dangerously." They both laughed and hand in hand went up to their respective bedrooms.

"I've gotta get some sleep," said Joanna "I'm on an early, otherwise I'd be in your bedroom with you celebrating."

"That's okay," said Josephine, "we'll do it another time. "'Night now. Hope you get some sleep."

15

The Assassin had boarded the last plane. They faced another twelve-hour flight. They had phoned ahead to a hotel near the airport so they could get a good sleep. They would spend a week there to be fully recovered then they would seek out a car rental agency and look for a four-by-four vehicle as they had been told the road to their destination was a long and very steep one. They felt that at last they were making some progress. Sebastian's Peak was looking closer at last. They would try to sleep on the plane. They had one more informer that the Agency had supplied them with who would give them their weapon and the address of their prey. They would not rush the kill. They liked to spend a few months in the area before they made their move. They needed to know how to make a fast exit from the address and that took time scouting out the area. They knew how to make themselves invisible. Besides a car they would also get a motorbike, but for now they'd try to sleep.

Captain Bedford was a very happy man. He had told all his Officers a few days ago that they would soon be launching another raid on Roger and Co. The message had obviously got through to them via Collins. What Collins didn't know was that Mitch had got one back to the Captain detailing which house Roger was now hiding in. Today would be the day the Captain would make his move. He had planned this strike very carefully. There would be snipers, the F.B.I., the C.I.A., the local Police and the Sheriffs from the towns who could be spared, all in on this. He had made the plans with them days before. They were just waiting for the heads up from Mitch. The Captain had rung them all at six a.m. to give them time to get the plan operational. He would tell his officers at seven giving nothing away to Collins. He'd keep him close. His officers arrived promptly at seven, knowing something would be going on but not what. The Captain emerged from his office and went to meet his officers.

"Today is the day of reckoning for Al's gang. Al was the head of the snake, Roger is the neck so I want Roger and the rest. Even as I speak Officers from the F.B.I. and the C.I.A. are moving in to target the houses we want. It's our turn to join the battle. Collins, Merton, Bayley, Thompson, Hain, Jefferson, Franks and Ginger, I want you all up front with me. Let's get started." The Captain picked up his foghorn. "This is the Police. Gang members, if you surrender yourselves you will not be harmed. Residents, please stay indoors no matter what happens. Stay safe indoors."

As he spoke, officers in protective gear were moving and surrounding the houses. They had especially got Special Ops on the house they knew Roger was in. The houses in question were now completely surrounded. Inside the house Roger was in he was barking out orders and assuring them it would be the same as before and that they'd win. Inside he didn't believe what he was saying as he could see officers outside in protective gear, surrounding them. He found himself completely at a loss for what to do for the first time. He mustered up all his strength to encourage all his men. They broke some windows and started to fire through them. They were met with gun-fire back and some snipers. The officers had broken windows of the respective house so they could fire back more effectively. They had been told to get Roger dead or alive. Bullets were flying everywhere. Many of the men in the houses had been killed. One house threw out grenades. They hit cars in the street and the cars flew up in the air bursting into flames and hitting some of the officers. Roger was panicking. He'd always won before. This was the first time he was not in control. All his information about his contacts was in the house. He would not surrender. They would have to kill him first. Snipers were picking off men who had smashed the windows in the roof. The Captain was losing men but this time they had got the advantage. The battle raged then suddenly stopped. The Captain waited and held up his hand to the nearest men, who passed it on. It was his way of saying "wait, be careful. Could be a trap". The men did as he'd ordered and waited. A few men started to surrender and were duly cuffed. The men in Roger's house were still fighting but they were low on ammunition. Bullets flew and were returned. One of the men told Roger they couldn't hold out much longer. For the first time in Roger's life he was out of ideas. Captain Bedford picked up the megaphone again.

"Give yourselves up and you won't be shot."

Roger began firing with the little ammunition that was left. He was met with bullets and one was a kill shot to the heart.

The men left there began to exit the house. Police vans were being loaded with cuffed men but most of them had been killed. The street was a mess with the burnt-out cars strewn over it. Captain Bedford sent men in to check Roger's house. They entered cautiously, guns at the ready. When they went in, they soon discovered that Roger was dead and the remaining men had given themselves up. They informed Captain Bedford. He was elated. Although Roger was dead, he knew there would be useful information in there. He would not let Collins go in there. Collins had performed well enough but he was still not trustworthy. He picked up the megaphone again, this time addressing the residents.

"Residents the fighting is over. You are safe now."

16

The Assassin had de-planed and got through the airport security okay. They had made a reservation for a hotel and were glad to find it was quite near the airport and from what they could see, so was the car rental. That was welcome news. They checked into the hotel and made their way to their room. They were tired but had slept some on the plane so they wandered over to the car rental. A salesman came over and asked what the Assassin was looking for.

"I'm going to Sebastian's Peak and hear I need a four-by-four."

"Sure do," said the salesman. "It'll take you two thousand miles. Then, when you get close to the end you start off on a straight road then it goes to thirty three percent incline, then you get fooled thinking it's over but it's not. You get the straight road again then the climb again and you do this six times. We call it the Roller Coaster. Once you've done all that believe me, you'll need a rest. So, a sister hotel to the one you're staying at is over the other side so you can get this one to pre-book a room for you. There are motels along the route. There's also another rental of ours on the other side, where you can check what you pick today in and choose a regular car."

"Is the road straight after that?" queried the Assassin.

"No, it's bendy in places but you'll find it does gradually straighten itself out."

"Do they hire motorbikes as well as cars?" asked the Assassin.

"Yes, sure do."

"Good to know," said the Assassin looking the vehicles over.

"Take a look and when you find one, we can go for a test drive."

"Sure, I'll get back to you." Having been in the Army, the Assassin knew exactly what they were looking for and soon found one for a test drive.

"You've chosen well," said the salesman.

"Have we got straight road to test on?" asked the Assassin.

"Some," said the salesman. The Assassin got in and fired up the four-by-four. She roared like a Hummer, eager to go. She ran like a dream and the Assassin could feel she had plenty of power to give. When they got back to the garage the Assassin paid for it to be reserved and made their way back to the hotel. Now they would rest. They were reaching their destination at last.

The Johnsons were feeling relieved, now that the gang had been taken down. Captain Bedford had told them that Forensics had moved in to all the houses to search for clues. They had been searching for his book of contacts and hit pay dirt when they found them behind a loose brick in the fireplace. The search would last some time, it was painstaking work. He was a happy man.

The Johnsons had invited Alex's parents to join them for lunch at a good restaurant in two weeks' time. Beth was wondering what to do about the weddings. Did Alex and Josephine want a small or large wedding? Did Alex have a large family? Did the girls want to get married at the same location on the same day? Should she get a wedding planner? Her head was spinning. She knew better than to worry. Nothing was solved by it. She closed her eyes and let peace enfold her. The key sounded in the lock a few minutes later. It was the girls. They were laughing together as they had when they were younger.

"Hi Mom", said Joanna. "We've been window shopping." They both giggled like school girls. "At wedding dresses," explained Josephine.

"So, did you find any you like?"

"Yes, we did Mom. The wedding store had quite a few we liked. We didn't try them on. We want you there for that."

Tears threatened to flow from Beth's eyes. Her voice sounding a little choked she said, "Well, we'll just have to do that soon won't we."

TWO WEEKS' LATER

The two families had enjoyed a good meal together. They found it easy to talk to each other and Beth was glad to find that they were not in any way 'stuck up'. The men were chatting amicably so the subject of the wedding fell to the ladies. Alex's parents were named Kelly and Steven. Kelly said that they were a close but small family and both Alex and Josephine didn't want a large wedding. This was good news to Beth's ears. They all enjoyed a good evening together and finally departed. Kelly had promised not to interfere with the wedding plans.

"Been there with our daughter."

On their way home both couples were chatting in their cars and both said how fortunate their son or daughter was to have such good in-laws.

The girls had taken two days off. They came back laughing and joking ready for their evening meal. Beth was home when they got there.

"We've been back to the wedding store. We've got pictures. Did you manage to get the day off Mom?"

"I did," said Beth. "I've not had a day off for ages but when I told them what it was for, they were fine about it."

"Good" said Josephine, you can help us choose our dresses and we'll help you choose your outfit."

"Sure", said Beth.

"We've sorted through the pictures and picked out some we like the look of in "A" line, said Joanna.

"That's a help," said Beth "we can have a look at them later."

The meal was nearly ready and Robert would be home soon. Sure enough, Robert let himself in. He soon saw that the evening would be for ladies only and went to his office once the meal was over. They had decided, with the agreement of Craig and Alex, that the Royal Hotel would make a wonderful location as it had a huge garden at the rear and huge rooms inside should it rain. It also had enough space inside as a venue for the reception whether it rained or shone. Beth agreed with their decision. "It's easy for the men," joked Josephine, "they only have to wear their tuxedos. Has Dad got one?"

"No. He'll probably hire one" said Beth. "Let's have a look at these dresses then." The girls had narrowed it down to two that they liked but these were just a few of them. Beth knew her girls. They would probably try on every dress in the store!

⊕

The Assassin had started the long journey to Sebastian's Peak. The four-by-four was running smoothly and made the journey easy. They were pleased. They had figured that it would probably be November time before they made the kill. Now, it looked as though it may be early October. They would bide their time though and if it took longer it didn't matter. Patience was why they succeeded. They had already worked out how far to go each day and pre-booked their motel listed on the brochure the sales-man had given them. They were on schedule and it felt good to be off a plane!

⊕

The next day the girls and Beth made their way to the wedding store. Because they were early there was no-one else there.

The assistant came up to join them and asked, "How can I help you Ma'am?"

"We'd like to see the 'A line' dresses please."

As she had thought, the girls tried on as many as they could until finally making their selections. Josephine chose a beautiful lace dress with cotton and satin lining it. It had lace shoulder straps and a 'V' neck. It dropped to the ground with ease, hanging to the floor beautifully. There was a slight 'train'. She was glowing in it. The assistant found a hand-made lace flower for her hair and a necklace of long pearls that completed the look.

Soon after, Joanna emerged in a chiffon dress that was hand beaded all over. It too had shoulder straps and a 'V' neck, and fell to the ground gracefully. Because it was hand beaded throughout, it needed no additional necklace. Beth told the assistant they would take those two along with the necklace.

"Now it's your turn Ma'am."

She was made to try on loads of outfits until the girls were satisfied.

"That's the one Mom," said both girls in unison. It was a light orange dress, with sleeves to the top of the elbow and a round neck. It fell just a short way from her ankles. The assistant brought out a matching jacket to complete the look. "Maybe a necklace of pearls around the neck?" offered the assistant. Beth tried some on.

"Yes," said the girls in unison.

"Right," said Beth to the Assistant. "We'll take everything we've chosen. I'll put it all on my credit card. When will you deliver?"

"Tomorrow."

"Can you make it the evening?"

"Certainly Ma'am, we'll do that. Here's your receipt. Thank you for shopping with us." Beth was worn out but the girls were still buzzing.

"Well at least we made a choice today. We don't have to go back again as some of our friends do," said Joanna.

"Yes," agreed Josephine. "We'll have to tell Dad all about our day. Where did you say we can get a good lunch Mom?"

"At the 'Ranch'. It's not far now."

The Assassin had driven five hundred miles and was ready for a break. They had pre-booked the first Motel along the route. That wasn't far now. The brochure they had been given also had a map folded in the middle, that opened out. That was useful. They had one more informer to see who would give them their weapon and the address of the Mark. The informer was in Sebastian's Peak. They had reached the Motel. Good. They would eat and rest and study the map.

17

A MONTH LATER

The wedding day had finally arrived. The wedding service was at five p.m. and their Pastor had been asked to do the traditional service. They had elected not to write their own vows as with their work schedule they didn't have time, but they knew how they felt about each other without doing that. It was a beautiful day so the service could be held outside. The day was extremely hot but by the evening it would be cooler. All the arrangements had been made and the Royal Hotel would host the wedding and reception. Limousines had been ordered and the wedding guests totalled three hundred. The photographer was due to come at four p.m., to discreetly photograph the girls as they got ready. It was half past three and the girls were getting antsy. Beth knew how they felt. She remembered her own wedding day. She had been the same. Time soon passed and the photographer arrived. The girls were getting into their dresses and would soon be busy with their make-up. Beth and Robert had gone to get changed.

"I'm so glad our girls have found good men," said Robert. "I feel a bit better letting them go knowing they will be well looked after."

"I feel the same" said Beth. "Could you do the zip up on the back of my dress please?"

"Sure."

"Let me do your bow tie Robert, you never can do that." They held each other and kissed then Beth did his tie.

The guests had arrived and soon all were seated. It was getting near five. The flower girls were busy scattering rose petals on the ground upon which Robert and the brides would walk. The grooms were in place and the Pastor was ready. Soon the wedding music began and everyone stood. The girls were radiant as they each held one of their Dad's arms. When they reached the grooms, the service began.

⊕

It was two weeks later and the Assassin had covered the two thousand miles and now had to face the 'Roller Coaster'. They had not been in a rush, pacing out their journey so as not to be overtired. After all, their Mark didn't know the Assassin was after them so there was no rush. They liked to get to know the area a person lived in before they made the kill. The last motel they had stayed at had told them to be careful as the Roller Coaster was dangerous. The Assassin valued their advice and believed their years in the Army would stand them in good stead. They had checked the vehicle over and all seemed to be well. They got out the burn phone to their contact and rang them. It was soon answered.

"I'm ready to collect my weapon and the Mark's name and address in approximately two hours. Where can we meet?" The contact told them. The Assassin put the meeting place into the Sat-Nav. "Okay I've got that. Are you at work at the moment or are you free?"

"Just got off from my shift at work. You picked a good time to call. I'll have everything ready for you."

"Okay, I'll call you again when I'm at the meeting place."

"Okay." They would dispose of the burn phone after the meeting.

The 'Roller Coaster' was every bit as bad as they had been warned. They started counting the hills until they finally reached the sixth, laughing their head off. The road then flattened out into a bendy, then straight road. They soon reached the meeting place and picked up the burn phone again. It was answered immediately.

"I'm here. Just over by the table in the corner." It was an old factory no longer in use by the look of it. The Assassin got out of the vehicle and went to meet their contact. "Hi," said the Assassin.

"Got your weapon and the name and address of the guy you're gonna kill."

"Okay, thanks. You're a cop?"

"Yeah, I inform to earn a bit more money."

"Is the gun loaded?"

"Yeah." For some reason the Assassin couldn't compute, it didn't sit well with them that the contact had turned out to be a cop. They had some integrity. So, they shot him. Collins would never inform again.

THREE WEEKS LATER

The Assassin had rented a car from the garage that was the sister hotel to the one two thousand miles back. They were also staying at the same sister hotel. They had driven around the area and had bought a copy of a local map of the area. They'd asked about a motorbike and were told that they could supply one. The Assassin had not looked around the area where Robert Johnson lived yet but a motorbike would make them more invisible with the helmet and leather gear. They would hire one and go take a look at the address after lunch. Lunch concluded, they had rented a motorbike with all the gear that went with it. They loved the freedom that being on a motorbike gave them. They took the coastal route to the address. They couldn't help admiring the scenery. It really was a beautiful place. They came to the address, took a fleeting glance then went on their way. They dare not stop as their neighbours would get suspicious. They had been sent by phone all the number plates of Robert and his family since they had been in Roger's possession. After Big Al's death Roger had given them to the lawyer, who in turn had sent them to the assassination agency. They hired a car today, and decided to follow Robert to work. They followed him carefully keeping well out of sight. When he reached his destination, there was a security guard outside. That meant there would be more inside, so they couldn't make the kill at work as they had with some businessmen. They would have to make the kill at his home by the look of it. That made it more awkward, since other family members would be involved. They had lock picks so they could get in and do the job and also a mask. They spent the rest of the day getting to know the area. They had a map of the area and were looking to follow all the roads that offered an escape route. They found two roads that did. When they got back to the Hotel, they got out a pink marker pen and marked the two routes.

TWO WEEKS LATER

The Assassin had followed Robert a few times to see if he went any place else apart from work. He didn't, so it would have to be a home kill. The Assassin hated those as they had to kill other family members too. This was to be the day, if possible, that they would make the kill. They drove to Robert's home and left the car four spaces back. They picked up the small bag that held the camera, the gun and the mask. It was the weekend and there were two other cars there. They checked their phone. Sure enough, it was family members. It was a nuisance, but they would have to deal with it.

The girls had come over as they had the day off, to show Robert and Beth the DVDs of their weddings. They were enjoying re-living it, laughing and joking, never suspecting what was to come.

The Assassin picked the lock and closed the door quietly. The hall gave way to a small room which could be entered from the hall and another door that gave way to the living room. There was a sofa that could hide the Assassin until they made the kill. They entered both doors and hid behind the sofa. They had a strange sense of déjà vu as they hid. They had no time for feelings They stood up, gun in hand, mask on and were stopped in their tracks by two faces looking up in fear, that were exactly the same as hers. She took off the mask.

"What's going on, I don't understand," she said.

"It's Eve, Robert, she's come back to us," said Beth.

"Put the gun down," said Robert quietly. But Eve couldn't. It was like an extension of her body.

"Sit down Eve," said Beth "and we'll explain everything to you. You're a triplet. A lady came into the hospital dressed as a nurse and took you away when you were two days old. It was on the hospital's CCTV. We did everything we could to find you but after five years we gave up. There was no trace of you in the States. Where did you grow up?"

"In England. They named me Angela. They always said an angel brought me to them. We moved back to Montana when I was six."

"These are your sisters, Joanna and Josephine. What are you doing here Angela?"

"I'm supposed to kill Robert for Big Al."

Robert spoke again, quietly, "Please put the gun down." She gripped it tighter, still having it aimed at Robert, then she lowered it but wouldn't put it down. Robert tried again and Eve-Angela lowered it to her left side.

"Were your parents good to you? Did you have a good upbringing Angela?"

"Yes to both those questions. I always felt that something was missing but never knew what. Now I know. I'm sorry for what I've become but it was do the kills or let them kill me."

"Please put the gun down." She still held it at her side like a cowboy's holster.

Sam had still been staying with them for a few weeks after the weddings. He was due to leave in the morning. He came down the stairs having had his morning nap. He entered the living room and all he saw was GUN! He was back in Iraq and an insurgent was threatening a family. He rushed at Angela and fought with her to get hold of the gun. Angela had at last been trying to put the gun down. The family shouted at him to stop, it was okay, but Sam couldn't hear them. He hadn't even noticed that Eve looked like the other girls. No, he had got to save this family. They struggled on and suddenly, the gun went off. Sam backed away and there was blood on his shirt but it was not his, it was Angela's. She fell to the floor. Instantly her sisters were on the floor to find out where she'd been hit. She had been shot on the right-hand side but it had nicked the aorta artery in the middle. The girls shook their heads. She would bleed out and have about five minutes to live. Beth got on the floor and sat near her head so she could talk to her.

Angela asked Beth, "am I going to die?"

"I'm sorry Angela but you are." Tears were flowing down her cheeks, she had wanted more time with her daughter.

"Then there are things I have to tell you. You have to make it look as though Robert is dead. There's a bag in your hall-room, you'll find all the instructions in the zip-up part inside the bag. The key-card to my hotel is in there. You'll get more info' there. You must take a photo of Robert, use my blood." She was getting weaker now as she was losing blood. Beth sat talking quietly to her, while Robert went to ring for the emergency services. Beth stopped talking, waiting for a response. Angela squeezed Beth's hand, weakly. "I would have liked to know you better," Angela looked at Beth, smiled at her, and then died.

"She once was lost, but now she's found," said Beth.

Then she started to cry. The girls were crying too, but went to get the bag where Angela had left it. They made Robert lay down and used some of Angela's blood to make it look as though he'd been shot in the head. They quickly took a photograph of Robert 'dead', then heard the sound of sirens outside. Sam was sitting with his head in his hands, crying and saying: "What have I done?" over and over.

EPILOGUE

The police had arrested Sam and taken him to the station. Angela's body was taken to a good undertaker. Once the family had got over the initial shock, Robert went down to the station and explained why Sam had reacted. They released him into Robert's care. The family found there were fake passports in the hotel. They'd found her current alias in the bag so they'd known to ask for Kate Anderson's room, having explained that she was their daughter and she had died. They did all that the instructions said, mailing the photograph of Robert in the stamped-addressed envelope. They buried Angela-Eve, under her given name 'Eve Johnson' so if anyone came looking for her, as an Assassin would, they would find no trace of her. The information in her things had made it clear what would happen if she failed. Angela had shot Collins so another Assassin shouldn't go any further in their search. The Agency would probably think she was on her way back, when she got killed, as the photograph had been sent in. So, the nightmare was over. They were safe now. Weren't they?.....

Printed in Great Britain
by Amazon